SNAPSHORTS

COLLECTED STORIES

THE HERTFORDSHIRE WRITING GROUP

HEATHER MUSSETT JACK DAVIS

CALUM DICKINSON

EMILY SIGGERS

STUART WAKEFIELD

TAYLOR MCLEOD

Snapshorts: Collected Stories

Book and cover design by Stuart Wakefield

Cover photograph by Suzy Hazelwood

INTRODUCTION

Every year on November 30th, the roller-coaster that is National Novel Writing Month leaves a group of Hertfordshire writers reeling.

National Novel Writing Month challenges us to write a fifty thousand word draft of a new novel in just thirty days. During that month, we encourage each other to meet the challenge but we're also part of a writing community we don't want to leave behind for the other eleven months.

I am one of those writers.

So we started The Hertfordshire Writing Group, an open, supportive community of writers across Hertfordshire dedicated to developing their writing skills and keeping each other motivated.

The meetings are always energetic, with new ideas and experiences shared, so when I suggested we put together an anthology of stories the answer was a resounding yes.

No two writers are the same and with that diversity came the need to find a common thread in each story.

We settled on ‘photograph’. Photographs make no sound, they are flat and silent. Yet they trigger memories, thoughts, and emotions that last a lifetime. Each photograph is a story, a fragment of a life lived. A moment of time, frozen in time.

I am delighted to introduce *Snapshorts*, The Hertfordshire Writing Group’s first anthology, showcasing the work of writers from across our fine county—and all committed to being the best they can be.

Enjoy.

Stuart Wakefield

If you’d like to find out more about National Novel Writing Month, please visit www.nanowrimo.org

If you'd like to find out more about The Hertfordshire Writing Group, please visit www.facebook.com/groups/hertswritinggroup

CONTENTS

IF I CAN'T HAVE YOU

HEATHER MUSSETT

Helen picked up a pile of photographs, haphazardly stacked, each one sliding over another. She fought to keep hold of them, but they fanned out and fluttered to the floor. Helen sighed, and leaned down with a groan to pick them up. Her fingers bashed uselessly against the shiny surfaces. Helen groaned again. *All I'm doing is moving them around.*

Her great-niece, Lucy, was sitting opposite her, helping her pack. She hadn't noticed Helen drop the photos, sitting with her hair tucked behind her ear, clutching a gilt frame and pursing her lips as she tried to guess who all the people in the photo were.

"That's you... oh, you had the same colour hair as mum, back then... And Granny Kate, with a baby...

is that you, mum? It must be, you're the oldest," Lucy pored over the photograph.

Anna, Helen's niece, leaned over Lucy's shoulder to look. "You're right, that is me," she said, and went back to packing Helen's clothes. She took down a periwinkle Jaeger silk blouse, stroking the material as she took it off the hanger.

They had been packing up all day, and it was now nearing tea-time. Her little Victorian cottage was emptying faster than an office at clocking off time. She was sitting in the nursing chair that had once belonged to her mother, next to her bed. She looked around, heaving a haggard sigh. Her carpet was strewn with boxes and packing paper, and her wardrobe doors were flung open, belching her clothes out in piles. Anna and Lucy were unearthing things even she'd forgotten she owned. How all of it was going to fit in a small care home bedroom, she'd never know. *Hopefully the room is as big as it looks in the brochure.*

Lucy flung the photograph in the box, pulling a face at the *crunch* from inside, and picked up the next one.

"Careful, Lucy, those are special to Auntie Helen!" Anna chided from the other side of the room.

Glowering, Lucy straightened the frame in the box and turned to the next one.

She peered at it, frowning. "Is that you and Auntie Liza?" she asked.

Helen, clutching the arms of the nursing chair for support, leaned over to look. It was the one she kept on her dressing table, taken in her early twenties. There was Ken, with his arm around her shoulders. She was leaning into his chest, beaming up at him, holding his hand. Liza, roaring with laughter, walked next to them. How loud, full of life they both had been, with her in the middle, letting them sweep her away.

"It is," Helen said. "Gosh, that was a long time ago. Help me pick up these, sweetheart." She waved her hand toward the photos she had dropped.

"What's next after these?" Lucy asked. She scooped them up and dropped them in the box. Helen blinked as Ken's face was covered.

Anna looked up. "You can move onto the rest of the dressing table. Just *be careful!*"

"I will," Lucy sighed. Her eyes slid over the perfume bottles and came to rest on Helen's jewellery box. It was white leather, and secured with a little brass lock. "Oooh! Have we got like, family jewels? Passed down for generations and guarded so they have to stay in the family?" She looked up at Helen, her little face bright with curiosity.

Helen chuckled. "Not quite, I'm afraid."

Lucy was already reaching for the lid.

"Lucy, there's no need to-"

But Lucy was already pushing the box open. "Look at these! Pearls!" She ran the beads over her hand, watching the sunlight dance over the iridescent surface. They clicked softly as they passed over her fingers.

"Come here, I'll put them on you," Helen said. She heaved herself to her feet and shuffled across the room, wincing as her hips creaked.

Lucy sat at the dressing table, grinning into the mirror.

"They make me look like someone off the telly, in a murder mystery," Lucy giggled.

"My mother gave them to me for my twenty-first birthday," Helen told her as she fumbled with the clasp. She tutted as the dainty silver slid out of her her swollen, stiff fingers. "She told me I was finally a grown woman." The clasp clicked into place, and Helen sighed with relief. *I certainly was more grown up than most girls my age by then.*

Lucy turned this way and that in the mirror,

rolling her shoulders as if the pearls were heavier than she expected.

"What's that?" she asked, diving down to the box again. She took out a velvet box, opening it before Helen could stop her.

Her breath caught in her throat. Anna shot her a worried look, so she arranged her face in the most relaxed expression she could.

"But, Auntie Helen," Lucy screwed up her face, frowning. "You weren't ever married, were you?" She held up the open box, puzzled. The ring, nestled in dusty satin, still glittered.

Helen couldn't help but smile at the confusion on Lucy's face. Her elderly great-aunt, in love? "No, darling, I wasn't."

"So why-" Lucy's eyes grew wide, her mouth a small "o" of surprise. "Did you *steal* this?"

"*Lucy!*"

Helen covered her mouth with her hand as she laughed.

"Lucy, you must be more kind with your words. Auntie Helen's fiancé passed away. It was very sad for her," Anna hissed.

"Oh, Auntie Helen," Lucy said, her shoulders sagging. "I'm so sorry." She bit her lip. "I didn't mean to upset you."

"Not to worry, darling, it was a long time ago."

Lucy looked down at the ring again, then back up at Helen. "You must have loved him a lot," she said. "Really a lot, to never have gotten married to anyone else."

Helen smiled, closing her eyes. "I did. I loved him ever so much."

The tapping and clicking of twelve typewriters filled the room, a wall of sound like the roaring of an engine. Helen glanced up at the clock. Two and a half hours left to finish three leaflets. Should be easy enough. She was sitting at her desk in the loft of a printing office, with the afternoon sun beating down on the back of her neck. The roof space was airy and bright, good for typing, but it was stuffy in summer. The foreman entered the room every now and then, leering out from under bushy eyebrows for anyone deemed not working hard enough. At the front of the room stood a large brass bell, the alarm for the start and end of shifts.

She smoothed her hair behind her ear. The trendy bob she'd had it cut into tickled her neck, but she had to admit it shortened her daily routine quite considerably. The other girls she worked with has oohed and aahed, lauding how the modern hairstyle suited her. Helen felt her cheeks warm at the memory. It was nice of them to say such lovely things about her.

Stay vigilant against the communist threat! She typed for the fifteenth time that day on the cover of the pamphlet. She sighed. There weren't any communists in Hull, surely. The news of the goings on in Germany made her shudder. She smiled, grateful that she'd be starting her family in good, safe, England.

When the foreman loped up to the front of the room to ring the bell, the metallic *clang!* jolted her out of her concentration. She raised her head, blinking.

"Come on, Helen, you don't want to keep your man waiting!" Teresa teased as she got up from her desk in the row in front.

Helen's cheeks warmed again. Sure enough, when she trotted down the wooden stairs and stepped out, blinking, into the setting August sun, Ken was leaning against a lamp post, smoking. His hair, dark as cola, fell in messy curls around his face, lifting in excited shivers on the breeze. His jaw, clean-shaven, was strong and square, but his lips were soft, curved gently around the end of his cigarette as he took a drag. His brown eyes lit up, his mouth curving into a lazy smile as he saw her. He pushed himself away from the post to stride toward her. He rolled his muscled shoulders as he walked.

"Hello," Helen said breathlessly, matching his smile.

He took a final drag on the cigarette and tossed it aside, waiting for Teresa and Molly to pass before he threw it.

"Hello, missus," Ken replied. He folded her into a tight hug, resting his chin on the top of her head. Helen burrowed her face into his chest, barrelled and strong from the shipyards, and breathed him in. This morning's soap and the sharp tang of sweat. And cigarette smoke. Helen wrinkled her nose.

"I wish you wouldn't smoke so many of those. They can't be good for you."

"Ah, now, that's where you're wrong," Ken draped his arm over her shoulders and they began to walk home. "It says so on the adverts. They've taken out the harmful stuff so you don't get a cough, and it's good for my digestion."

"It's not good for mine, that smell makes my stomach turn," Helen pushed him gently, smiling.

"It's all for you, baby," Ken sang, making the

elderly couple walking ahead of them turn and frown at him. "So, how was your day?"

The next morning, a new girl started in the typing pool. She bounced into the loft, a minute before the bell, looking around for a spare seat. The girls in the row in front began whispering behind their hands, eyeing the new girl's buttercup yellow patterned dress and lime headscarf.

"That's very current," June said from next to Helen, her eyebrows disappearing up into her fringe.

A thump and creak from the stairs told them that the foreman was on his way up.

"Come and sit here," Helen said, gesturing to the empty chair on her left. The new girl grinned and sat down. Helen kept an apron on the back of her chair, which she grabbed and passed to her. "Just so he won't make any comments," she said, nodding toward the stairs.

The new girl raised an eyebrow, but took the apron and finished tying it just as the top of the foreman's head appeared at the hatch.

"Same job as yesterday, carry on, girls," he called before he'd even entered the room. "Ah, good, you're here." He glanced at the new girl. "Helen can show you the ropes. I need fifty pamphlets by lunchtime. Don't let me down!"

The girls settled to their work, rolling their eyes and pulling faces at his retreating back.

"I'm Liza, by the way. Thanks for this," the new girl gestured to the apron. "He seems a bit of a pig."

"He's not the nicest," Helen said. She took the top pamphlet from her pile from the day before and passed it to Liza. "This is what we're working on. Do you need a hand to-"

As it turned out, Liza didn't need Helen to show her any ropes. Her typewriter was already set up with fresh film and paper loaded, and she was leafing through the pamphlet, skim reading. She scowled.

"Complete rubbish," she spat.

Helen blinked.

"Stuff like this is just as bad as what they're doing in East Germany," Liza rolled her eyes at the pamphlet, as if she expected it to apologise and rewrite itself.

Helen pursed her lips.

Next to her, June looked alarmed.

"So, are you new to the area?" Helen asked, turning to her own typing.

Liza answered without moving her fingers from

the keys, looking up to smile at Helen. "Yeah. I've moved up here from London so I can save up to move to San Fran."

Helen frowned. "San Fran?"

"San Francisco. California, the United States of America. They've got the right idea."

June cleared her throat.

Helen had heard about the hippies in San Francisco. Ken said they sat around not doing much, smoking things much worse than cigarettes. Helen trained her face to look politely interested.

Liza looked up and laughed. "Have I shocked you? I'm sorry, I tend to do that. Let me guess: you're going steady with your local sweetheart and can't wait to get married and have hundreds of babies?"

Helen flinched. Was there anything wrong with that?

"Aren't you a good little housewife. Go on, tell me about him. Is he just like Elvis Presley?"

"I'm hearing too much yapping and not enough tapping!"

Helen jumped at the foreman's voice booming up the stairs.

Liza pulled a face toward the stairs. She carried on, her voice lowered. "So, go on, tell me about your sweetheart."

When the foreman called them for lunch, Liza led the way to the courtyard, pulling a packet of cigarettes from her bag.

Helen fiddled with the cross around her neck, running the pad of her thumb over the engraved metal. The other girls descended.

"So brave to wear that colour," Teresa said. "Harry would have torn you to shreds if you hadn't covered it with that apron."

"It's just a dress," Liza shrugged.

"What was that you were saying about America?" Molly asked.

"I'm a singer," Liza explained, closing her eyes in relief as she took a drag on her cigarette. "I want to go out there and join a band, travel the world."

Molly laughed. "And I'd like to go on a date with Paul McCartney, but here we are working in the same typing pool."

"Nothing stopping you going to Liverpool and giving it a try," Liza said.

Molly laughed, but tailed off as she realised Liza was serious. "A future like that isn't for us sort of girls," she said.

"If that's what you believe," Liza shrugged.

Helen sipped her tea, watching Liza talk. Everything from her auburn hair, worn long like a Bond girl, to the smoke spiralling from between her fingers was so... *modern.* She believed everything she was saying, regaling the girls in the pool gathered round her like disciples. June was the only one who sat apart, her lip curling in disgust.

Later, when they'd finished for the day, Liza beamed at her and thanked her for looking after her. Pulling her bag onto her back, she set off toward town.

"Who's that?" Ken asked.

"She's new. Absolutely bonkers," Helen breathed. "She says I showed her the ropes but she didn't need it at all. I've never known anyone so confident."

"Maybe she can teach you a thing or two," Ken smiled down at her.

"She wants to join the hippies in America."

Ken winced. "Maybe don't let her teach you about that. I'd like to keep you all to myself."

Helen giggled. "I can assure you, Mr. Taylor, that there are no worries on that account." She looked down at her cross again. "But maybe God put her in my path for a reason."

• • •

Helen studied her reflection in the mirror. The rose pink of her tea dress set off her English rose complexion beautifully, and when she put on the matching hat waiting on her nightstand, she'd look just like Jackie Kennedy. She smiled, pressing her hand to her stomach to stop the butterflies. She didn't know how she was going to eat a thing.

She and Ken were going for a picnic in East Park. Just the two of them. Helen couldn't quash the excited giggle that rose in her chest.

Don't get too excited, she told herself. *It could just be a nice day out.*

A knock at the door. Her father answered it. Helen flew down the stairs, grabbing her hat as she went.

"You're wearing a tie!" she exclaimed. "What's the occasion?"

Helen's heart beat faster. *What if today really is the day?*

Ken coughed, covering his mouth with his hand. "I just wanted to make an effort for my girl, that's all. Is that allowed?"

"Of course it is," Helen replied, smiling up at him as she took his arm.

East Park was busy with families enjoying the late summer sunshine. Ken strode purposefully to the top end, away from the children screaming in joy as they queued for the slide. He chose a shaded spot under an ash tree, throwing out a blue tartan blanket to sit on. He stood and looked at Helen, wringing his hands.

"Is this OK?" he asked.

"Perfect," Helen breathed.

Ken pulled at his tie, then nodded to himself.

"I'm sorry, I can't put it off any longer," he said, dropping to one knee.

Helen's heart leapt. *It's happening!*

Moments later, there was a ring on her finger and tears were streaming down her face. She clung to Ken, squeezing him for all she was worth. The moment she said yes, the tension melted out of him and he stood up, beaming. The ring was a little large, but he'd be able to resize it for her, he assured her. She told him it was the most beautiful thing in the world.

"Now it's official," Ken smiled, cupping her face with his hands. Helen looked up at him, in love with each tiny detail, down to the smallest eyelash. He bent down toward her and pressed his lips to hers.

"Just like in the pictures," Helen said.

"I'm so glad you said yes," Ken sighed, flopping onto the blanket on his back.

"Did you really think I wouldn't?"

"If you have something precious, you always worry about it."

He reached into the picnic basket and pulled out a bottle of Babycham. "One day, I'll be able to afford to buy you champagne," he said. "For now, I hope this will do."

The bubbles in the drink glittered in the sunlight, just like Helen's ring. She admired it again, a small solitaire diamond, dainty on her petite fingers. She couldn't wait to show the girls at work.

Oh, what a good little housewife.

She smiled, imagining what Liza would say. She wouldn't say anything unkind, would she? Would Helen care if she did?

"So, I'm thinking of a nice little terraced house in Sculcoates. Near to our families but not too close."

"That sounds lovely," Helen replied. She nestled herself under his arm.

"And children. One of each?"

"I don't think we get to choose!"

"It'll be our perfect life. Of course we get to choose."

"If you say so," Helen said, laughing.

Ken gave a short cough into his handkerchief

before lying back on the blanket, beckoning for Helen to lie with him.

On Monday morning, high pitched squeals of delight filled the air in the typing loft.

"Oh, it's beautiful!"

"How did he do it?"

Helen blushed. The focus was on her, and only her, even though Liza's headscarf was today a brazen red.

The door banged and the girls jumped, scurrying to their seats.

"What's all the fuss about? I've never heard such a damned stupid noise," Harry snarled. He hadn't shaved that morning, and his eyes were wide and bloodshot.

Helen kept her eyes down.

"No, really, what's all the fuss?"

Harry glared around the room.

"Helen's gotten engaged," June offered.

"Oh, really? Let's have a look," Harry strode over to where Helen sat, towering over her with his arms crossed.

Helen looked up at him. Her heart thumped. She held out her hand to show him.

"Ah. A ring. So how long until you leave us to start popping out babies?"

Next to her, Liza sucked in a breath. Helen opened her mouth to reply, anything to head Liza off from saying something stupid, but Harry carried on, his voice echoing around the loft.

"In the kitchen, and raising children. Helen's doing it right!" He looked around the room at the young girls clustered at desks. "You all have no business being here. You're all just killing time until a man decides to put you out of your misery and take you off the shelf."

Helen gasped.

"How dare you be so bloody rude," Liza spat.

Helen's heart dropped.

"Helen might stay. She might want to earn some of her own money once she's married. God knows that house prices are high enough, and strikes at the dockyards are more and more common."

Harry turned to face her, his eyes narrowed.

"What sort of bullshit leftie point of view is that?" he sneered.

Liza held his gaze, thrusting out her chin.

Helen willed her to sit down, to back down and leave him alone.

"Politics has nothing to do with it. Helen deserves your respect. She at least made the effort to look presentable to come to work."

Harry scowled, his eyes glinting in spite. He looked Liza up and down, his gaze resting on her hair.

"Oh, yes, some of us did make an effort this morning, didn't they." He sauntered closer to Helen and Liza's desk, hips swaying as he leaned back. "You're even wearing red. Is that why you're here, eh? To keep an eye on what we're doing?"

Liza's mouth twisted in disgust.

Please, God, don't let her say anything stupid, Helen begged silently.

Liza looked Harry up and down. "I'm just here to do my job," she said.

Harry laughed. "And don't you forget it."

He turned on his heel and stalked back down the stairs to the offices below.

Slowly, the stunned silence was overcome with startled whispers and the clunking of typewriter keys.

"You didn't have to do that for me," Helen hissed.

"I didn't do it for you. I did it for all of us. He can't speak to us like that," Liza spat in reply. She jabbed at the typewriter keys with a savage energy. She stopped. "Although, I might not have bothered speaking up if it were June he was chewing out."

Helen didn't know what to say to that, so she nodded, let go of her cross, and got to work.

For the rest of the week, both Helen and Liza kept their heads down, tapping out word after word, page after page.

After work, Helen's family asked her if she and Ken had set a date, where they would be living, who was going to be making her dress.

That Friday night, Liza invited her out to see a local band.

"That sounds great," Helen said. "What do you think, Ken? Do you want to come along?"

Ken stood next to her, his arm draped around her shoulders. She leaned into his familiar warmth, basking in the glow of being surrounded by her favourite people. She frowned. Was Ken breathing quicker than normal?

"They're fairly new, I don't know how good they'll be," Liza shrugged. "But if they are, maybe they'll let me sing with them."

The labour club was buzzing with people, the men with pints in hand, the girls clutching gins. The band hadn't started yet, but their instruments were on stage already, stand-ins in the spotlights before the show came to life.

Liza had brought a Polaroid camera.

"Take our picture," she called to one of Ken's friends.

Helen stood in the middle, Ken's arm over her shoulders, Liza's arm around her waist. She smiled.

The air was filled with the shouts of laughter, booming voices fuelled by drink and bravado. Ken saw some friends from the shipyard and took Helen over to meet them.

"Oh, so here she is, the mythical Helen!"

The man pulled her in for a kiss. His breath stunk of cigarettes and booze.

Ken, returning from the bar, coughed, putting the hand holding his lighter over his mouth. Once the fit had subsided he stood for a second, breathing heavily.

Helen looked up at him. "Baby, are you OK?"

"Absolutely fine," he grinned. He passed her a gin and lime. Helen gulped down the cold drink, savouring the chilling ice against her teeth. The room was warm. Ken shouted and laughed beside her, slopping his beer on the floor. She smiled up at him. His eyes gleamed and he seemed to grow inches taller the more the group laughed at his jokes.

Helen finished her drink and Ken went to get her another one, leaving her with the group.

"He only did it to get his end in, and he ended up delivering lace for weeks!" a friend yelled, slapping his leg as he laughed.

Helen smiled weakly. The room seemed to be moving in slow motion. She leaned her back against the wall, steadying herself.

Where was Liza?

She looked around and saw her sitting alone at a table in the corner. Helen stood up and battled her way over, apologising as she bumped and lurched off elbows and backs.

"Hello," murmured as she reached Liza.

Liza sat slumped against the cheap plastic chair back, arms folded, glowering.

Helen settled herself next to her. "Are you all right?"

Helen thought Liza wasn't going to answer, she was glaring so fixedly at the floor. She took a breath to ask again when Liza responded.

"It's just shit," Liza exploded.

Helen jumped, looking around them expecting to see heads turning and raised eyebrows, but the noise in the room masked Liza's outburst. "What is?"

"Just, life! Everything about it!" Liza spat. "I don't

want to get married and have babies. Fine. I want to wear what I like and go where I like and-" Liza swallowed. "*See* who I like, you know?" She grimaced. "But that apparently makes me too different."

Helen groaned. "Just ignore Harry. He's got a power problem."

"Can you blame him? He's in power!"

Helen nodded. She couldn't think of anything to say to that. She blinked, forcing her eyes to open again as she swayed in her seat.

"You've got it so easy," Liza continued. "I've tried wanting what everyone else does. Truly, I have. But in the end it's just... not what I want."

"You wouldn't be you if you wanted what everyone else wanted," Helen replied. She nudged Liza with her shoulder. "That's what makes you so beautiful."

"Why can't everyone be like you, Helen?" Liza smiled, closing her eyes. Helen flushed with pleasure.

Helen watched her friend. She really was beautiful. Stark against her pale, porcelain skin, Liza's cheeks glowed red. Her dainty mouth was pouted in frustration. A crazy thought came to Helen, and before she'd had time to think about it, she was acting on it. Helen leaned down and lightly kissed Liza's cheek.

Liza opened her eyes.

Helen flinched. *What did you do that for?* She must have had too much gin.

Their eyes met. Helen searched Liza's face for any sign of hurt, or anger, or embarrassment. Instead, all she saw was an odd calm.

Helen's mind was running at double speed. That wasn't an abnormal thing to do, was it? Friends kissed friends all the time. Her best friend was upset, and she was comforting her. There was nothing more in it.

Their faces were, all of a sudden it seemed, awfully close. Helen pulled away, sitting back up again.

There was a scuffle near the bar.

"Oh my God, he's not conscious!"

Helen turned to look. All Ken's friends were gathered next to the bar.

Her heart dropped, icy cold.

She stood up and ran to the bar, clattering off chairs, wincing as bruises bloomed but skidding her way to the group.

"Helen, he just dropped..."

Ken was on the floor, crumpled as he'd fallen.

A hand on Helen's shoulder. "James has gone for a payphone."

Helen nodded. Why had he fallen? He hadn't had that much to drink, had he?

Please, God, let him be OK. Don't do this to me.

Ken coughed, the muscles in his back straining against his shirt. Groaning, he pushed himself up onto his elbow.

"Ken, your mouth!" Helen breathed.

Frowning, he wiped the trickle of blood from his chin. His lip was split from the fall. "Was I in a fight?" he asked breathlessly.

"The ambulance is on the way," said James coming back from the payphone.

"Come off it, I don't need to go to hospital," Ken said.

"You're going to hospital whether you like it or not," Helen growled, more harshly than she meant to.

You should have been there with him.

Helen gulped.

Liza touched her shoulder. "I'll stay with you as long as you need."

"No, it's OK," Helen gabbled, recoiling away from her. "You don't want to sit in the hospital all night. I'll see you tomorrow."

Liza frowned.

Immediately, Helen felt awful for flinching away. Liza hadn't done anything wrong, and neither had she. She had to get a grip of herself. Ken needed her.

"Honestly, I'll be fine," she smiled, squeezing Liza's arm. "I'll see you tomorrow."

7 a.m. came and went. Helen should have been at work for 9 a.m., but that time passed her by as well.

Face creased with worry, her mother brought her a cup of tea and set it on her bedside table. It grew cold as Helen continued staring at the ceiling, remembering the night before.

"How many cigarettes do you smoke per day?" the doctor had asked, frowning over his clipboard at Ken.

"About twenty," Ken replied, his voice hoarse.

The doctor pursed his lips, tilting his head in admonishment as he looked at Ken. "You know that's very bad for you, don't you?"

Ken rolled his eyes.

"We'll have some tests to do, but we can't rule out that it might be a chronic lung condition. You might have to live with this for the rest of your life."

Helen cleared her throat to make the words come. "Sorry, doctor, but what does that mean?"

The doctor turned to look at her, eyes wide in surprise. "It means that your fiancé could end up very sick indeed, I'm afraid," he replied when he'd recovered himself. He put his hand on Helen's shoulder. "You should get cracking on that wedding planning."

Helen felt as though she'd been slapped. Get cracking on the wedding planning? But that meant...

Ken's father had dropped her off at her parents' house and she had gotten herself into bed without cleaning her teeth or putting in her curlers.

And there she still was, lying in her bed, staring at the ceiling.

What was she to do? What if Ken died?

What if it's your fault?

Helen squeezed her eyes shut. *Don't think that, that's completely ridiculous,* she told herself. Liza was her friend, nothing more.

Jesus thought that Judas was a friend, too.

Her heart sank.

Is this all my fault?

Tears spilled out from between her eyelids. *I'm just overtired,* she told herself. *Get some rest.* She'd be up for visiting time in the afternoon.

Later that afternoon there was an insistent tap at the front door. In her dressing gown, hair undone, Helen padded through the hall to answer it. She flinched. It was Liza.

"You said you'd be at work today, and you weren't. Don't worry, I told Harry you were sick and you couldn't get through on the telephone." She stopped to look at Helen and frowned. "Oh, no. Bad news?"

Helen shook her head. She leaned on the door frame and closed her eyes. "Not yet. But it could be."

"Is that the kettle I hear boiling? Good, let's get some tea on."

Liza stepped up into the house and marched Helen back through into the kitchen. Helen let herself be steered, tripping over her feet as she walked.

"Sit down," Liza said, pointing at the kitchen table. She made tea, now and then asking where the mugs were, the tea bags, the sugar.

"I don't take sugar," Helen said.

Liza dumped in two teaspoons anyway. "It's good for shock. I suppose you haven't eaten all day?" She turned to Helen with her hands on her hips.

Smiling despite herself, Helen shook her head.

Helen watched the steam pitch and swirl out of

her tea cup before it evaporated into the air. So pretty, but so fleeting. She welled up again, pulling her tissue out of her sleeve and dabbing at her eye.

Liza reached over and took Helen's free hand. "Whatever it is, I promise I'm here to help you with it. You won't be alone."

Helen sighed. She let her fingers lie limp in Liza's hand. She wanted comfort and she appreciated Liza being here, but she didn't want to make matters worse.

"I've got to go back to the hospital soon," she said.

"I'll drive you," Liza said.

"Oh, don't worry, I was going to walk."

Liza looked her up and down. "I don't mean to offend you, but you might frighten Ken if you walk into the hospital looking like that."

Helen looked down at herself. There was a tea stain down her front, one of her nails was broken and she was already irritated by the loose hair she was having to tuck behind her ears.

"Let me drive you. It'll give you time to get ready."

Helen sighed. She did have a point. And since when had it been a sin to let friends look after you?

It was a week before Ken's test results came

back. Ken was much better and brighter, pacing up and down the ward.

"If they let me go home today," he said, striding toward the window, "I can be back at work on Monday and I'll only have lost a week. It won't be that bad." He smiled at Helen, his eyes glittering. "This won't be too much of a setback."

Helen smiled back. His optimism swept her up as well. He looked fine - so he was fine, surely?

The doctor walked into the ward, his shiny patent shoes clicking on the floor. He took off his glasses as he reached them, shaking Ken's hand and nodding politely to Helen.

"Maybe you should step away," the doctor said, taking Helen's hand in both of his. "I need to speak to Kenneth on his own about some rather complicated things."

Helen nodded. "Of course, doctor. Thank you for all your hard work."

She walked away, toward the corridor, and sat down. She frowned. Why had she let him steer her away? Now she had the painstaking wait.

Liza wouldn't have let the doctor send her away.

Helen's stomach dropped again. Why did everything come back to Liza? She hadn't done anything wrong. God was doing her a favour by bringing

Ken's illness to light as soon as possible, before it got too bad to treat. And anyway, it wasn't going to be anything truly horrible. Look at Ken, look at how strong and healthy he looked.

He had his back to her, but his shoulders were tense. Helen smiled to herself. He always screwed up his shoulders when he was concentrating. The doctor was probably using all kinds of wordiness Ken wouldn't be used to.

Minutes later, the doctor stood up and walked toward her. He nodded, giving a thin smile, then carried on up the corridor to his next patient.

Helen stood up. Ken was still sitting where he had been, his chin resting on the palm of his hand. He was staring out of the window, his breathing shallow.

"What's the news, baby?" Helen asked as she reached him.

"The doctor said I have lung cancer," Ken said, frowning. "But how is that possible?"

Helen's face fell. Lung cancer. Cancer. *Cancer.*

"What do you mean?" she asked, clutching for something to hold onto.

"He said I should stop work," Ken replied.

"But you look fine."

"I still need to work."

Both of them sat, dazed, Helen staring at the floor, Ken out of the window. Helen only moved when then nurse came with Ken's medication.

"Doctor will come and do a home visit in a week, to check how you're doing."

Ken nodded, not looking at the nurse.

The following Monday, Ken went back to work, and Helen started volunteering with the church association.

Marjorie, the leader of the Women's Institute, couldn't thank her enough. "It's so lovely to have some young blood in the group," she said. "Come and see my delphiniums, I'm saving them for the Easter Sunday flowers."

They all said what a dear she was, smiling knowingly at her ring, telling her long winded stories about their own engagements. Helen listened, smiling in all the right places, filling her time stitching knee rests, arranging flowers and ensuring that the Sunday school had enough cake for the break time.

Ken carried on as usual.

The moment Helen arrived back to the typing pool, the girls descended.

"Liza told us what happened..."

"Is Ken OK?"

"Should he be back at work so soon?"

"You're still getting married, right?"

Helen smiled, sighing with the effort of putting on her brave face yet again. "Of course we're still getting married. Ken is going to be absolutely fine."

Liza waited for her at the desk they shared. Helen smiled, pleased to see her. She ignored the pang of dread. Liza leaned back into her chair, looking at Helen with an eyebrow raised.

"What's that for?" Helen asked.

"Who are you trying to fool?" Liza asked back. "You said he's got lung cancer. That's bad, Helen. People die. He needs to be looking after himself.

"And how do you know he isn't?" Helen snapped. "He feels fine. He is fine. There's been some kind of mistake. People like Ken don't get cancer."

Liza raised her eyebrows and turned to her typewriter. "And healthy people don't collapse because they can't breathe," she said in an undertone.

"What are you trying to say?"

"I'm trying to tell you to stop lying to yourself and give yourself a break. You'll never beat this if you don't acknowledge there's a problem!"

Helen gasped, staring aghast at her friend.

"I'm sorry, that was harsh of me. I just don't want to see you get hurt, sweetheart."

Helen dropped her gaze. "I can't make him rest. I can't make him believe that there's anything wrong. Soon I'll have to start carrying him home. It's awful, Liza. I don't know what to do."

The tears came again. Hearing Harry's heavy footsteps on the stairs, Helen quickly wiped them away.

"Oh, for the love of Christ," Harry howled.

Helen flinched.

"First you go off sick without telling me, now you come into work blubbing." He stamped over to her, leering over her with a half smile. "Something wrong with your husband-to-be?"

"That's a horrible thing to say, and you know it," Liza growled.

"Ooh, you've got your little hippie friend standing up for you now, have you? Planning a nice little trip to Moscow together, are you?"

"Stop being so foul!" Liza screeched.

"You can both get out of my loft. Both of you. I haven't got time for hysterics today."

Helen looked up at him, aghast.

"I mean it! Get out! And come back in tomorrow with workers' heads on! Bleeding hell, you'd think lefties would have better work ethics," Harry grumbled as he moved away.

"Come on, Helen." Liza took her arm and dragged her out of the room, glaring at Harry as she went.

"But, today's pay!" Helen squeaked. "You need it for your travel fare!"

"One day won't make a difference. I wasn't going to stay there and listen to him spewing hateful rubbish like that."

Out on the street, Helen stopped. "What are we going to do? I can't go home, my parents will kill me."

"We're having a day off," Liza growled, her face set. She took Helen's wrist and dragged her along the street.

"Liza!" Helen stumbled along behind her. "Where are we going?"

"You'll see in a minute," Liza replied. She kept up a furious pace, and Helen was soon puffing with the effort of keeping up with her.

Finally Liza slowed outside the local cemetery. Marble pillars reared up around them, joined by a spiked black iron fence.

Helen scowled. "Thank you for the reminder, Liza."

"No, that's not what I mean." Liza pushed open the heavy gate and led Helen inside. "Look at these."

The graves were arranged in lines, leaning at angles where the ground had shifted over time.

"Liza, I don't understand."

"Read these."

P. K. Galletley

Loving husband and father, creator of empires.

And

His beloved wife, M. Galletley.

Helen frowned. She moved on to the next one.

S. T. H. Smith

Loving husband to his wife, also buried here.

"Don't you see?" Liza asked.

"They're all buried together," Helen said. "It's romantic." Her vision blurred. *I'll just have to wait longer than most.*

"This woman didn't even get her name recorded!"

Helen looked at the gravestone again. The word "wife" was covered in lichen.

"Is this what you want your life to be?" Liza asked.

"If it means I've shared in love, then yes! Why wouldn't I?"

"You have so much to offer, Helen! Why would you want to reduce yourself to one line on someone else's headstone?"

"It wouldn't be his headstone," Helen mumbled. "It would be ours."

"You're missing my point." Liza shook her head, scowling in irritation.

"You're not making a point," Helen said. "All you've done is remind me that my fiancé might die!"

"What I'm saying is don't die with him!"

Helen flinched as if Liza had slapped her. "That's what love is, Liza. I'm sorry you've never experienced it, but that's what you do when you love someone. You share everything with them, even the bad things."

Liza stared at Helen, her eyes searching Helen's face. "I have experienced love," she said in a small voice.

"Well, in that case, you should know," Helen snapped. "I'm going home." She turned on her heel and stomped back toward the gate. She fumed. How *dare* Liza make assumptions like that about hers and Ken's relationship. Liza must know how upset she was. What was she playing at bringing her here?

"I'm leaving this weekend," Liza called after her.

Helen stopped. Her stomach dropped. It felt like Liza had punched her. "What?"

"I wasn't going to tell you until I was sure you would be OK but," Liza swallowed, then picked up her sentence. "But now you've made it clear you'll be absolutely fine, I'm perfectly happy to tell you I'll be in San Francisco by Monday morning."

Helen blinked, recovering. She steeled herself to say something, anything. "Well. Safe journey, I suppose." She stepped toward Liza with her arms out, but Liza stepped away, shaking her head.

"Go and look after your fiancé," she said. "But just think - who's going to look after you?"

Helen closed the gate behind her when she left. Her first thought in reply to Liza was: *well, God, of course. And my parents.*

Ken was getting worse. He had to stop for breaks to catch his breath on the way home, and on the day that the doctor was due for a visit, he had such a strong coughing fit, clutching his mouth with his hand, that he grabbed Helen for support. Helen clutched at him as his entire body shuddered with the wracking coughs. She buried her head in his shoulder. "I wish you'd smoked less," she cried into his skin.

The cough subsided, and Ken rested for a moment, breathing heavily.

"Me too," he breathed. He wiped the blood off his hand on his work trousers.

Both Helen and Ken sat quietly, contrite, as the doctor gave Ken a sound talking to. He needed to stop work. He needed to take his medication and he needed to rest.

Ken nodded, not speaking.

After that, the fight went out of him. He wasted away, his cheekbones protruding and his hair hanging in lank strands over his face.

Helen moved into Ken's parents' house to help care for him.

"We see you as our daughter in law already, sweetheart," his mother said.

Helen cried.

Her last day at the typing pool was the same as Liza's.

"I hope it all turns out well for you," she said squeezing Helen's arm.

Helen flinched away from her, then caught

herself. The last thing she wanted was to hurt Liza's feelings any more. "And to you," she smiled. "I hope it's everything you dreamed."

When she got home that night after helping Marjorie with the Easter flower arrangements, she fell to her knees, burying her face in her bedspread, and sobbed. She keened and wailed, gasping for breath as her misery flooded out of her. One best friend was dying and the other was on her way to the other side of the world. Soon, she would be alone.

And it's all your fault!

She smacked her coverlet with her fist. "Why am I being punished?" she wailed into the blankets.

Helen jumped at a hand on her shoulder. She looked up to see Ken crouching beside her, wiping a tear off his face.

"Come here," he said, pulling her onto his lap. The pull was feeble, but Helen knew what he meant. She turned, draping her legs over his, and tucking her head into the crook of his neck. It had become hard and bony now the weight had fallen off him. Helen took a deep, shuddering breath, timing her breathing with the beating of his heart. It seemed to echo in the cavity of his chest.

"You aren't being punished," he murmured.

Helen felt the vibration of his speech rather than heard it. "You're being given an opportunity to prove your strength. And I know how strong you are."

He took a breath, but it caught in his throat and he coughed softly. "When I'm gone, don't let yourself be lonely. Let other people look after you."

"Now, are you sure you're going to be OK? You have everything you need?" Helen followed Anna, nodding as she inched her way to the door.

"I'm sure I'll be quite comfortable. Thank you for all your help, darling," Helen smiled as Anna pulled her into a hug.

Helen waved them out of the room, assuring them that she'd be fine, she was sure she'd be quite happy, and please do come and visit her soon. She shut the door and paused with her hand on the doorknob, staring at the thin, white painted wood.

The decor of the room was dated: textured floral wallpaper in pastel rose and sage green, a cream carpet and gilt handles on the doors. The furniture jarred in that veneered way, medically designed beds and chairs doing their best to look domestic and not quite managing. Helen sighed. *Just because I'm old, it doesn't mean I've lost my sense of style.*

In the corner was a small kettle on a tea table, just like in a hotel. She wandered over. What else to do but make a cup of tea? She was sure the room would start to feel like home before too long.

The photo of her, Ken and Liza was on her bedside table. She gave a wry smile. *Thank you, Lucy.* Helen shuffled over and picked it up. How calm, carefree, and *well* Ken looked. Her stomach clenched in sadness. How different would her life have been if Ken had been one of the lucky ones? He had died not a month later, and Helen had been alone. She went back to work, not at the typing pool, but for a local shipping co-ordinator. She organised the diary of the managing director, keeping the sales teams in line. She half-smiled, remembering how, when she was younger, they would compete to see who would be able to get her to go out with them. Of course, none of them were successful. Later, when her hair had faded to white and her wrinkles began to deepen, they saw her as a mother figure.

It was a long time since she'd been attractive to any man.

There was a knock at the door, and without waiting for an answer, the door opened.

"Here's my good little housewife. You're here! And of course you've already got the kettle on."

Helen beamed.

Liza still wore her usual headscarf, tied close and covering her scalp. Her eyes still glittered with mischief through her wide rimmed glasses, and she stood with both hands on her walking stick, a satisfied smile spreading across her face.

Helen poured out tea into two cups. "You know I could never be without you."

SHOOT THE KILL

JACK DAVIS

January 30th, 1968

Saigon sure was a hell of a lot louder than back home in Virginia.

As Martin rushed to work, buttoning up his shirt and pushing his hair to the side as he bolted out the door, the South Vietnamese capital's orchestra assailed his ears. The engines of a thousand motorbikes, the cries of mama sans selling fresh fruit from their bikes, and the constant honking of horns blasted through the city, as relentless as the heat in summer. A choking smell of gasoline, incense, cooking meat, spices, and cheap cologne mixed together in a sickly-sweet perfume that hung in the thick, humid air and Martin couldn't help but smile.

Sure, Saigon was chaos. It was a city thriving on corruption, decadence, and a misguided faith in the American dream but Martin loved the damn place. He'd begun to find an odd beauty to the hustle and bustle of the city, the electric energy in the murky metropolis, and the toothy smiles of the locals. It was his own personal playground.

And the best part of it was, the war would never touch him here.

Martin crossed a street, bikes and motorbikes weaving past him as if he were a rock in a stream, and pushed through a gaggle of robed monks collecting alms.

"Sorry!" he cried out, pressing his palms together like he'd seen the locals do. But he had no time to seek their forgiveness. He had a goddamn job to get to. Speaking of which, he pulled his camera out and took a quick photo of the monks next to the traffic.

What a shot!

Martin dived down a side street and passed a bar that was blaring out a vicious Hendrix guitar lick. He noticed a buxom go-go dancer who was lighting up a cigarette in the dark doorway, the brief flash of light highlighting the soft features of her pale face. Christ, she was a beauty! What a photo she'd be.

Martin looked down at his watch, noticed how early it was in the day but how late he was running, and pushed the image of the girl out of his mind, pressing on down a dingy alleyway. He clutched his bag a little closer, sparing a glance at a dark-dressed man leaning against a lamppost.

Turning the corner again, he came at last to the headquarters of the Greensburg Daily Herald in Vietnam, and made his way through to the editor's office. He knew the drill. Two knocks on the door, a packet of cigarettes thrown on the desk, and Martin was ready to take his seat. It was only then that the thick heat of the capital began to soak the underarms of his shirt. He cast a longing look outside.

"You're late," Zachary Kent snarled, spinning in his chair to face Martin. The lines in his leathery face sharpened as he looked at Martin in disgust.

Martin looked down at his watch. "Sorry, sir," he said, hoping his apology sounded convincing.

"I don't like how you've been acting lately, Compton," Kent said. "How long have you been in country?"

"A year, sir," Martin said. "Same as you."

"And what have you done in that year?" Kent

scratched at his salt and pepper moustache, leaning back into his chair. He picked at the peeling leather on the arm rests.

Martin frowned. “What do you mean, sir? I’ve taken photographs.” He pulled out a brown folder from his bag and placed it on the scratched desk.

“You’ve taken photographs.” Kent sighed. “You’re in Vietnam and all you’ve done is taken photographs of—”

A motorbike screamed past outside, followed by a tirade of angry Vietnamese.

Kent slammed his fist. “It’s like goddamn gook city out there!”

“Well to be fair, sir, we *are* in Vietnam.”

“Ain’t that the goddamn truth.” Kent pinched the bridge of his nose. “Where was I?”

“We were talking about my photography, sir.”

“Yeah. Your *photography*.” Kent narrowed his eyes. “Well, what the hell are you doing in Vietnam?”

“I came here with you, sir,” Martin said and paused in thought. Vietnam *was* pretty far away from Virginia. A hell of a lot more dangerous, too. “Say, sir, what the hell are *we* doing in Vietnam?”

“Don’t you start with me, kid,” Kent said. “That’s all I goddamn hear in Saigon. They all ask me, 'Kent, what the hell is a small town newspaper doing in Viet-goddamn-nam?' I say to them, 'What the hell is a small town newspaper *not* doing in Vietnam?!'"

Martin shrugged loosely. "That's fair enough, sir."

"We're going to put Greensburg, Virginia on the map my boy." He tapped a finger on the desk. "*That's* what we're doing in Vietnam. The Greensburg Daily Herald is making movements, boy, here in Saigon. So what the hell are you taking photographs of in Vietnam?"

Martin stared blankly at the editor. "Sorry, sir?"

"What are these photographs?" Kent picked up the brown folder on the desk and picked out a few photographs. He tossed them at Martin.

"Slice of life, sir." Martin said, grabbing one of a couple of Vietnamese teenagers laughing on a street corner. One of them was carrying a Rolling Stones record and was wearing a pair of aviators that he'd told Martin a pilot had sold to him for two dollars. Not a bad deal, all things considered, and it was a pretty little photo, Martin reckoned. He smiled, proud of the shot, and remembered how one of the girls had been a little too eager to be photographed. Poor girl probably just wanted some money. Thought Martin's photo would be her way out.

"Slice of goddamn life?"

"Slice of life, sir." Martin nodded. "Showing Greensburg what life's like in Vietnam. For the Vietnamese." He smiled.

"Greensburg don't care about the gooks!" Kent threw his hands up in the air. He sighed and opened the packet of cigarettes, pulled one out, and lit it with his zippo. "Hell, who the hell cares about the gooks anyway?" Kent handed over a cigarette and lighter to Martin.

"Well, we do, sir," Martin said, lighting the cigarette in the corner of his mouth. "That's why we're in Vietnam, right?"

"We're in Vietnam to show Greensburg what the war's really like," Kent said, waving a hand about and filling the room with cigarette smoke. "Show the people of Greensburg blood and bullets and mud and trenches and helicopters and dead soldiers and dead civilians." He coughed, spat to the side, cleared his throat, and stuffed the cigarette back between his chapped lips. "That's what Greensburg wants to see."

Martin swallowed hard, the bullets, mud, trenches, helicopters and dead bodies flashing through his mind like he'd seen on the seven o'clock news. "That's all a bit graphic, sir," he squeaked and took a deep drag from his cigarette.

"That's the point!" Kent said. "I don't want no photos of gooks sitting about in their funny little hats, smiling at you, drinking coffee or riding bicycles. Hell, I don't care for 'em. You remember that photo of the burning monk?"

Martin's face went pale. Malcolm Browne's horrific photo was etched into his mind, the flames twisting around the sitting monk who looked so calm, so at peace. He simply nodded.

"Well I want fifteen of the robed bastards burning alive." Kent jabbed a finger towards Martin. "Caught on your camera," he snarled.

The cigarette drooped in Martin's mouth. "Sorry, sir?"

"We need to show the world what's really going on in Vietnam," he said. "And you're going to be the man to do it."

"Me, sir?"

"You, kid." Kent nodded. "You and your photographs. Used to be a war overseas was too far away for Doris back home in the States. But now, she sees it all, just like she's squatting next to the GIs herself in some backwater jungle near the

Cambodian border. Hell, she can almost smell it! And what she sees starts changing her mind. She sees things that she don't rightly like in the paper, she tells her husband, and that gets *him* thinking about what's going on here in Vietnam. And if enough husbands start thinking about Vietnam, then things start to change." Kent paused to clear his throat and took another drag from his cigarette. "And who publishes all those photos? The Greensburg Daily Herald. We're sorted for life , and we're out of Vietnam." He grinned, tendrils of smoke escaping from his lips.

Martin looked down at the desk, knitting his eyebrows. "But it was your idea to come to Vietnam in the first place, sir."

"No it was not," Kent said. "I ain't the President."

"That's true, sir," Martin said, hoping Kent would soon send him on his way back out into the streets. Back into the beautiful city. Martin could almost taste the bánh mì and smell the sweat and perfume. He thought back to the go-go dancer as he slid his photos back into the folder. She sure would be able to strike a pose.

"So get me some photos, kid," Kent said. "I want fighting, I want guts, I want blood!"

Fighting? Guts? Blood? Martin dabbed the sweat

away from his brow with a quivering hand. "You sure, sir?"

"Sure as shit, kid." Kent nodded. "But there's a problem at the moment."

"Yeah?" Martin hoped the problem was big enough to buy him more time in the bars of Saigon, a problem big enough that he would still be able to take photographs of the pretty locals and the beautiful colonial French architecture without hopping on a huey and going into the jungle. To see the fighting, guts, and blood. Martin's Vietnam was no war zone.

"There ain't much fighting outside of Khe Sanh at the moment," Kent said, tapping his cigarette on the rim of a glass ashtray. "There's a ceasefire because of Tết."

"Tết, sir?"

"It's like Chinese New Year," Kent said. "But Vietnamese."

Martin frowned. "Right, sir."

"So I'm sending you to Khe Sanh." He pulled out a map of Vietnam and stretched it across the length of the desk, knocking the ashtray on the floor, and swore, blaming it on the heat.

"Sorry, sir?"

"Khe Sanh." Kent pointed it out on the map.

"Right by the border with —" He paused, rubbing his temples. "How the hell do you pronounce this country anyway? Laow? Louse? Hell, why don't they use some goddamn proper American names? Sure would make things a hell of a lot easier. Call it... Lee or something. God's very own American hero. God rest his soul." He snorted. "General goddamn Lee. Where was I?"

"Khe Sanh, sir."

"Khe Sanh!" Kent said. "Gooks have broke their own ceasefire. Of course they have. They ain't got American sensibilities. All that rice must go to their heads or something, I don't know!"

Martin rolled his eyes and took a drag from his shaking cigarette to try and calm himself down. He'd heard what was going on in Khe Sanh on the radio. And it didn't sound good.

"I want you to go there and take photos of all the blood and guts," Kent went on. "I want a marine crying out for his mother as his innards are spilling out. I want people burning alive in their choppers. I want Gook civilians being shot by grunts in the heat of the moment! The army's counting a high body count and I want all of the dead sons of bitches on camera."

“All for the people of Greensburg, Virginia, sir?” Martin asked.

“For the goddamn United States of America, kid!” Kent pointed at Martin with his cigarette. The ash on the end dropped off, landing on the spot marked ‘Saigon’, and began to burn. He slapped away at the smoke and tossed the map to the side. “This is bigger than Greensburg, Virginia. Hell, it’s bigger than Richmond! Bigger than Virginia!” He paused, frowning a touch, and shook his head. “Ain’t nothin’ bigger than ol’ Virginia.”

“Texas, sir,” Martin blurted out.

“Texas?”

“Bigger than Virginia, sir.” His cheeks reddened. Why the hell had he said that? He looked down at his shaking hands.

Kent scoffed. “The good American people ain’t seeing enough of Vietnam.”

“It’s all over the news, sir.”

“And what good and patriotic American watches the *news*? The future’s in print, my boy. The future’s in the Greensburg Daily Herald. So we’ll publish our photos because the American people need to see what this war’s all about so we can get it over with and get back home, away from these goddamn communists, these goddamn gooks, and their goddamn food."

Martin looked across at the smoking map. "Don't you want us to win the war, sir?" he asked.

"Of course I want us to win the war," Kent said, leaning back in his chair.

"But you want us to leave Vietnam?"

"I don't want us to lose the war."

"But aren't we winning the war, sir?"

Kent nodded "For now." He coughed and took a long drag of his cigarette. "I want you off to Khe Sanh tomorrow morning?"

"Tomorrow morning?!" Martin's voice cracked.

"I'll arrange transport for you," Kent said, picking up the receiver of his telephone.

"What if I can't get any photos, sir?" Martin asked. He pulled out his camera. "What if this stops working? I ain't taken it outside of Saigon, sir. Not quite sure how it'll—"

"You'll get the photos, Compton," Kent sneered. "Or you're on the next plane back home to the States and you're fired! Now get the hell out of my office and send in that zipperhead that sorts us out with the coke. I'm goddamn parched."

Martin stood up, dusted down his trousers, and hurried out of the office. He passed the young Vietnamese paperboy who waited in the hallway and jerked a thumb towards the office. "Boss wants a coke, Duck," he said, trying to hide the trembling of his voice, before slipping back out into the streets of Saigon.

"It's Duc!" Duc called out behind him.

But Martin didn't give a damn.

Martin passed through the streets of Saigon in a delirious daze, ignoring the late morning hazy heat and the taxi drivers offering him weed and cocaine. He was sweating buckets by the time he arrived back at his apartments, and staggered up the stairs.

But John Wayne blocked his way.

John Wayne was a mean old bastard who could stop any man dead in his tracks with a choice side eyed glare, but looked nothing whatsoever like the film star. Still, the nickname seemed all too appropriate for the squat Vietnamese lady who Martin had been cursed with as his landlady. She was as fierce as any of the cowboys Martin had watched in his childhood's films.

John Wayne put one hand on her hip and held another out. She barked something in Vietnamese.

Martin looked at her blankly and shrugged. "No

Vietnamese!" he said. "*Désolé, Mademoiselle—Madame! Désolé*!"

"*Où est le loyer?*" she asked back but Martin slipped past her and darted into his room.

John Wayne didn't speak a word of English and Martin never had wrapped his head around Vietnamese, so Martin had come to a unilateral decision to communicate exclusively with her in broken French. It had worked out well at first, but Martin's high school French only stretched so far when John Wayne hammered on his door demanding his rent that was a week late.

Hell, maybe if he died in Khe Sanh, he wouldn't need to pay this month's rent. Martin swallowed hard. Oh Christ, it was all starting to feel a little too goddamn real.

Collapsing onto his bed, Martin could have burst into tears. He just wanted to stay in Saigon! Saigon was safe, Saigon was cool. Saigon was a place where a man could do whatever he wanted if he pulled the right strings and flashed enough dollar bills to the desperate locals who loved anything and everything that was wrapped up in the star spangled banner of the red, white, and blue. He didn't want to be among marines and grunts and machine guns and helicopters, near the heat of napalm and the deafening crash of rockets and grenades and God only knows what else. The only thing that came wrapped up in the American flag out of Khe Sanh was a damn coffin being lowered into the ground. And Martin reckoned he was owed a couple more decades on God's green earth before he'd allow himself to succumb to being swallowed up by the mud below.

He sat up in his bed and pulled off his shirt, leaving it in an ever-growing pile of laundry in the corner of his room, and fished out a tasteless Hawaiian shirt from his wardrobe. Buttoning it up, Martin examined himself in the mirror, and ran some pomade through his fair hair. He tried to smile at his reflection but just felt his stomach churn. Khe Sanh? Khe goddamn Sanh?

Christ, Martin needed a drink.

Something strong that could help him forget about Khe Sanh. Everything he'd heard made it sound like hell on earth. And he was in his own heaven here. He didn't want to be in a war. Hell, that wasn't why he'd come to Vietnam. Martin sure as hell wasn't a soldier. Even in Saigon, hearing the choppers in the distance gave him the creeps. The thought of being somewhere in the world where you could be happily alive and breathing one moment and dead the next terrified him. Just how many had died in Vietnam now? Too many, he knew that at least. And Martin didn't want to end up as another statistic. He was more than that. He was an artist, a master of his craft. If there were guns and grenades and grunts firing at Vietnamese peasants dressed in their finest pyjamas, then Martin sure as shit wouldn't be anywhere near.

He didn't care for this war, nor for the poor bastards fighting in it. It wasn't his scene. It wasn't who he was. He'd leave all that to the professionals, the boys who'd been trained to drill and march and run and shoot and kill, and everything else soldiers got to do. Martin wasn't a soldier. He was a photographer, a photographer who enjoyed the finer things in life. Like not being shot through the neck, blasted away by a grenade, or lying in the mud with his legs blown off.

The little things.

And if not wanting to die in war made him a coward then sure, Martin was glad to be a coward. Anyone who wanted to die in this country was mad, and Martin always prided himself on his sanity.

So why the hell was he *still* in Vietnam? Martin had thought that his idea to go to Vietnam with the Greensburg Daily Herald to escape the draft was one of the best ideas ever concocted in the history of

Greensburg, Virginia. How could the government send him to fight in Vietnam if he was already there? The past year, he'd indulged in all the pleasures Saigon had to offer and hadn't regretted a thing. But all that could be ripped away by the bastard Zachary Kent.

Kent would fire him if he didn't get those damned photos he so desperately wanted. And getting the photos meant being in the action, in the thick of it, deep in country amongst the poor bastards the President was sending halfway across the goddamn world to fight a war they didn't care about. Martin sighed. He supposed his luck had run out. A year spent in Saigon hadn't been wasted, and he always knew that eventually he'd have to join some unlucky company of soldiers and see the war for himself. Perhaps it'd even make for some interesting stories for back home?

Christ, Greensburg seemed so far away.

Well, it was, really. Nine-thousand miles away. Martin was nine-thousand miles away from Virginia, from his home, his family, from his father.

God damn that man.

He sure was pleased to be away from Colonel Richard Compton, with his dreadful regulation buzz cut, his pristine dress blues he always wore whenever he wanted to show off how much he loved the country he had fought for, his study decorated with more American flags than a Fourth of July parade, and his sneering dismissal of any career that didn't involve shooting foreigners who were supposedly threatening his God given rights, democracy, *and* the constitution.

"Why don't you just do your bit?" his father would always ask at any family dinner. "I did my part at D-Day, and I'm a better man for it. And remember your grandfather? The army made him the man he was, and there ain't no finer man in the world than your grandfather. Of course his father before him served his country too, and your great-great grandfather fought for the Union in the Civil War, you know..."

When news of Vietnam had become a daily feature in the papers, radio, and on television, Martin's father had become even more unbearable, yapping on about the domino theory, and why Martin should sign up this instant to serve out in the Far East, and how jealous he would be of Martin's service out in Vietnam, for Martin's father had missed out on the chance to be shipped to Korea and he'd always wanted to fight the Asians. Any man who didn't sign up to fight in Vietnam was, in Colonel Richard Compton's opinion, a goddamn communist. Worse, he was a coward. And he would never tolerate a coward living under his roof.

So Martin had gone off to Vietnam to escape the draft and shut the old man's trap right up. It was still too early to go home. And hell, Martin was glad to be out of Greensburg, Virginia. Nowhere on earth was as dull as Greensburg. All he had to do was prove to his father that he wasn't an unpatriotic, communist-loving coward.

But Martin rather enjoyed being a coward if it meant he was still alive. It paid to be a coward in Saigon, far away from the fighting. And hell, he'd probably even loved a communist or two. Just communists who liked dollar bills and knew exactly what to say and exactly how to dress. Communist or not, those girls had to make a living, he supposed. And better working under bed sheets than Ho Chi Minh.

Khe Sanh.

How the hell would Martin survive Khe Sanh?

Martin looked at himself in the mirror, straightened his hair, and slung his camera over his shoulder. If this was going to be his last night in Saigon, he sure as hell wouldn't be spending it alone in his room, wracking his brain with thoughts of his father and his own mortality.

Better to do that with a pretty girl with a few dollar bills in her bra.

He left his room and was greeted by John Wayne again, who burst into rapid and angry French, demanding rent, respect, and Christ only knew what else.

"*Desolé! Desolé*!" Martin cried out as he left the building. "*Je vais*, uh, *la guerre! Au revoir!*"

John Wayne gasped and held a hand to her heart. Good. Let her think Martin was off to be a hero in the war. He wouldn't be no hero, and he wasn't going to war as a sober man. So Martin found a bar and ordered several glasses of whisky and a couple bottles of beer, and spent much of the night dancing with the girl he'd seen with the cigarette this morning.

As he lay with her in a drunken stupor, he somehow managed to hold back the tears, cursing his father, the war, and Zachary goddamn Kent until he passed out.

January 31st, 1968

Martin was woken up by the sound of fireworks and firecrackers nearby. He felt around beneath the covers, noticing he was alone in the bed. Frowning, he scrambled about finding his watch and cursed the Vietnamese for celebrating at two in the morning. The firecrackers were pretty damned loud. Martin sat up in the bed, wiped the drool from his mouth, and pulled his clothes back on. The cold loneliness of the rusted wire bed made him feel shameful, and he just wanted to go back to his apartment. He trudged down the stairs, placed a fistful of dollar bills on the bar and stepped outside.

And realised all of hell had come to Saigon.

Martin heard that dreadful sound, the sound that had given him the chills whenever he'd been taken to the range as a kid with his father, the sound he never wanted to hear in Vietnam, the sound he'd been trying to avoid by staying in Saigon.

Rat-tat-tat-tat.

Rat-tat-tat-tat.

Brr-rat-tat-tat-tat.

And in the distance, but far too close for comfort, a terrifying *kaboom*.

What the hell was going on?!

Saigon was safe. Saigon wasn't home to war. Saigon was a beautiful haven! So why the hell was the night sky lit up with red tracers? Why could he hear rockets and grenades exploding in the distance? Why were his ears wracked with the sound of machine gun fire? The fighting was in the rice paddies, the villages in the middle of the jungle, on hills far away from cities. That fighting had, quite rightly, stayed out of Martin's life.

But now it was *here*?! There was no escaping it! Martin felt his heart in his throat and looked down at his shaking hands. His skin was slick with sweat, his breathing was short and shallow, and he had a frightful feeling in the depths of his stomach. He was at fucking war!

Martin ran for his life. This wasn't his scene. He didn't want to end up as another statistic, a bodybag on the plane home, a headline in the Greensburg Daily Herald.

> ***Local Photographer Dead in Vietnam*** *- more on page 7.*

That wasn't how it'd end. It couldn't end here in Saigon. Not in the darkness of the early morning. Nothing was supposed to end in Saigon. Saigon was a beautiful beginning, a paradise of women and bars. Maybe Martin could still make it back to his apartment and wait things out, whatever things were. Maybe it was another coup? The army had overthrown President Diệm four years ago, after all.

He adjusted the sling of his camera and ran as far as he could, legs pumping and lungs burning, his breathing ragged as he turned a corner. Despite the darkness, Martin could still make out the smoke rising above the buildings of Saigon, flares lighting up the sky, and no matter where he seemed to run, he couldn't escape the metallic din of gunfire and the spine-chilling boom of explosions.

Rat-tat-tat-tat-boom-tat-ka-ka-ka-boom!

Jesus Christ in goddamn heaven, just what the hell was going on? There was supposed to be a damned ceasefire! So much for Tết!

Martin came to a stop on some street corner and leant against a wall, trying to catch his breath. He looked around and realised he had no clue where he was.

It was dark, he was afraid, and he wasn't thinking straight at all!

Martin swore under his breath and carried on down the road he was on, hoping he'd be able to find some landmark. Buildings were on fire, and he could hear desperate shouting in Vietnamese, the fizz of flares, and the crackling of rifle fire. It was as if the sky had cracked open and the earth itself was shaking.

But Martin had to keep running, he had to keep going. He had to get home. And so he did. He ran for what felt like hours, diving down streets and alleyways, and running away from where the sounds of fighting were loudest. Everything hurt and he just wanted to get home. Back to his bed, the sweet safety of his bed. Hell, he'd even take John Wayne's cursing over this!

As he pictured the angry, wrinkled face of his landlady, Martin stumbled down a street and froze, his breath caught in his throat. A group of shadowy figures turned towards him.

"VC?!" A voice called out in the darkness, and Martin heard the click of a safety switch.

He threw his hands up. "American!" he cried, his voice cracking. "I'm American! Don't shoot! Please!"

Several orders were hurriedly barked in Vietnamese and a short man in a green military uniform came rushing over to Martin.

"What are you doing here?" the Vietnamese soldier asked Martin. He looked frighteningly young and his tanned skin was covered in all manner of nicks, cuts, and grazes. Large bags hung under his eyes and he had an M16 slung across his chest.

"I'm trying to get back home," Martin said.

The Vietnamese soldier flashed a smile. "Back home?" He snorted. "You're a very long way from home, American."

"No, I live in Saigon," Martin said. He looked at the soldiers in the murky darkness of the early morning. "Can you help me?

The soldier adjusted his sling and hefted his rifle. He nodded once. "Come with us." He turned back to his men, said a few more orders in Vietnamese and beckoned Martin to follow along.

Martin sighed. He only wanted to know where the hell he was, not accompany a goddamn group of Marvin's through the streets of Saigon.

But then he got an idea. A little niggle that grew in his mind, a seed that had been planted, watered, and had sprouted in the heat of the Saigon sun.

Kent wanted Martin to take photos of the real war and now the war had made its way to Saigon. He looked down at his camera, cleared the dust from the lens, and followed the ARVN soldiers, hoping that he'd be safe with them.

And to think, he'd come damned close to pissing his pants a few moments before. He looked down.

Dangerously close.

"Do you know what's going on?" Martin caught up to the group of soldiers and asked.

"Saigon's being attacked," the soldier who had spoken with him said.

Martin rolled his eyes. "Yeah, I gathered that." He sighed. "It's the VC?"

"I think so," the soldier said. "You a soldier?"

"No," Martin said, looking down at his Hawaiian shirt and camera around his neck. "I'm just a photographer.

"Can you shoot?" the soldier asked.

"My camera, sure."

"No," the soldier said. He tapped his rifle. "Gun?"

"I'm not the best shot," Martin said, grimacing.

The soldier shook his head and muttered something to himself in Vietnamese. The squad continued down the street and turned a corner, and Martin cringed as the sounds of gunfire got louder.

Up ahead was the Presidential Palace. Martin had taken a couple of photos of it when he'd first arrived in Saigon, and had marvelled at the all-white building. He'd got a great shot of the South Vietnamese flag flying in the wind. Now, the building was lit up by flares and rockets that careened through the skies. The metal gates were open, the grass lawns pockmarked with craters, and the muzzle flash of rifles firing nearby punctured the morning darkness. The enemy had stormed the damned building. The soldier issued frantic orders to his men to get down, and gestured for Martin to take cover next to him by a parked car. A radioman came over, and handed the headset over to the soldier in command. He spoke into the receiver. Martin didn't understand the words but saw the soldier was swearing profusely.

"More are coming," the soldier said, radio in his hand.

"VC or you guys?"

"We guys."

Martin flinched as rifle fire broke out from the palace gardens. Some of the soldiers around Martin opened fire themselves. "I'm Martin, by the way," he said to the soldier in command, raising his voice above the gunfire. "Martin Compton." He held out his hand.

The Vietnamese soldier looked down at it, then to the palace, and finally back at Martin with a quizzical look on his young face. "Nguyen Tran Quang," he said. "*Thiếu tá*, uh, major."

"Major?" Martin widened his eyes. "Ain't you a little young to be a major?"

Nguyen shrugged. "Maybe. I've been fighting for a while. I'm good."

"I'm sure you are."

Nguyen pressed the radio speaker to his ear and nodded along as a crackled voice came through. He muttered something in response.

"We, err, we got it all under control?" Martin asked.

"No." Nguyen said.

Martin wrinkled his nose. "Alright then." He leaned against the car and looked down at his camera. Peering over his shoulder, he tried to frame a shot that would make even Kent blush, but the light was far too poor.

"Why are you a photographer?" Nguyen asked. "Not a soldier?"

Martin furrowed his brow. "Never really thought it was my thing to be honest," he said. "I mean I'm thankful for guys like you but..." He bit his lip. "My whole family were soldiers and I guess I didn't want to follow along."

"My whole family are soldiers too." Nguyen said with a slight smile. He popped his head over the car and looked over at his men who had all stopped firing. Sporadic gunfire erupted from the direction of the palace and Nguyen slinked back down behind the car.

"That so?" Martin asked.

"My father fights—" Nguyen paused and corrected himself. "*Fought* against the Japanese. He was Viet Minh."

Martin perked a brow. "Like Ho Chi Minh?"

"Yeah, like Ho Chi Minh," Nguyen said, bobbing his head up and down. He adjusted the straps of his helmet which dangled on either side of his face. "He led the Viet Minh in the war against Japanese."

"So you're Pa's a communist?" Martin cocked his head.

"No!" Nguyen shot him a harsh look. "He's not communist. He works for government."

Martin looked down at the camera in his hands, blinking. That didn't mean he wasn't a communist. "Why did he fight *for* Ho Chi Minh?" he asked, looking back up at Nguyen. "I thought Ho Chi Minh was a communist."

"He fights because he wanted his home to be free," Nguyen said. He waved a dismissive hand. "You Americans don't understand."

"Well we fought to be free," Martin said. "Hundreds of years ago, I suppose."

Nguyen grunted and silence fell on the two. Martin was glad to be free of not having to give an

American history lesson to the young Vietnamese major and looked over at the palace again, feeling sweat run down his brow. He was really here. In the goddamn war. At any moment, some VC sniper could take aim at his head and fire, popping his skull like a damned cherry. He quickly ducked, terrified.

"What do you think of Ho Chi Minh?" Martin asked to try and forget the fact he was, now and somehow, on the front lines. There was something about this little Vietnamese major that intrigued him and even calmed him. He'd never spoken to a soldier for this long before. Or at least not over a beer in a dimly-lit bar.

"Ho Chi Minh?" Nguyen paused. He didn't seem to mind having a conversation in the middle of a war zone. His voice was cool, calm, and collected. Martin felt a strange pang of envy for the man's bravery. Then again, only brave men got themselves killed in war, and Martin was not looking forward to being shipped home in a bodybag.

"Well he did a lot of good," Nguyen said after a while. "Freed us from the Japanese. He makes a lot of sacrifices, has no family. That's... That's big."

"Huh." Martin swatted a fly from his face. "So you like Ho Chi Minh?"

Nguyen shrugged. "I just want Vietnam to be

safe again," he said and looked over to his men. All were in cover waiting for who knew what. "No more fighting."

"You're not a communist then?"

"No, of course not," Nguyen said, rolling his eyes. "I am just Vietnamese."

"So you don't care about fighting communists?" Martin asked, his curiosity getting the better of him. He was glad Nguyen was humouring him, at least.

"Well, the communists have done many bad things," Nguyen said, hands tightening around his rifle. "They threaten my family, they threaten my home. That's why I fight them. Not because they are communist. How many Vietcong read Marx?"

Martin breathed a short laugh at that. "Have you read Marx?"

"At school, yes," Nguyen stated.

Martin frowned. "You went to school in North Vietnam?"

"No. In Paris."

He blinked. "And you read Marx? In Paris?"

"Yes," Nguyen said. He looked again at the palace and scrunched his face up.

" ... Do you believe in communism?" Martin asked.

"I don't think so," Nguyen said. "What does it matter anyway?"

"Well you're supposed to be fighting the communists," he said.

"But I don't care about fighting communists," Nguyen said. He looked down a street to the right. "I just want to keep my family and country safe," he said, turning back to face Martin. "Japanese, French, communists. It doesn't matter who they are. If they threaten my country, I will fight them."

Martin didn't want to bring up the Americans. "But what if you die?" he asked instead.

"Then I die," Nguyen said, far too casually for Martin's comfort. "I want to do my duty. Like my father did. Like I should do. My country is very... Broken at the moment. I want to help fix it."

Martin leant his head back on the car, perplexed at Nguyen's sheer dedication to his duty. It was alien, foreign, and damned crazy. This kid would willingly die for Vietnam? Martin doubted if he'd ever want to *die* for the States. He could do so much more being alive. And he rather enjoyed being alive. If Martin died for his country, would the President even care? Would he lose sleep that another life was gone in 'service' to the United States of America? Hell, at the rate this war was going, the President better be a damned insomniac. Martin just couldn't understand this poor bastard.

"How long you been fighting?" Martin asked. "In the army?"

"Four years," Nguyen said. "I join up as soon as I turned eighteen."

"Wait, you're twenty-two?" Martin's jaw hung open. "And you're a major?" The kid was a couple years younger than him for Christ's sake! *And* he was determined to die for his country after fighting? He looked into the boy's eyes and shuddered. He hadn't seen it before, but Martin's own eyes had adjusted to the darkness, and he could see the tiredness in Nguyen's eyes, the bloodshot, distant, tired eyes. It was a terrifying sight. If this is what Kent wanted the people of Greensburg to see, the true toll of war on a goddamn kid, then this was Martin's damned duty.

To Martin, Nguyen was the damned face of this whole war. Just how long had Vietnam been at war again? Since the Japanese invaded? Longer? This poor kid's life had known no peace. But could that even be captured on camera? Could a photograph show what twenty-two years of war did to a poor bastard like Nguyen? Could a photograph show the blasé indifference Nguyen had to dying for his country? The kid who went to school in Paris could be snuffed out at any moment out in the jungle. Hell, not even in the jungle but here in Saigon! Martin would try to do his best. He took his camera in hand. "Say, can I get your picture?" he asked.

Nguyen stared blankly at him "What?"

"Can I take a photo of you?"

Nguyen narrowed his eyes. "Why?"

Martin shrugged. How the hell could he put his mad thoughts into words? "I'd quite like to," he simply said.

"Okay?" Nguyen adjusted his helmet and straightened himself, sitting up slightly. Martin crawled back and looked at Nguyen's face in the viewfinder. In the harsh light of the flares in the sky, it looked as if it were carved out of stone. Martin turned the focusing ring, placed his finger over the shutter release and pressed down.

Click.

BANG!

A gunshot rang out and Nguyen fell down, blood spurting out from his skull. It was as if he was a puppet, the strings cut.

"Jesus Christ!" Martin recoiled and fell onto his back. He scrambled around on the floor, dragged himself away from the car and ran. He didn't have any time to think, no time to mourn, no time to pay his goddamn respects. His pulse was faster than a damned machine gun.

Rat-tat-tat-tat.

Brr-rat-tat-tat-tat.

The image of the bullet tearing through Nguyen's skull, the blood spraying from his head, the harsh, brutal speed of it all, was imprinted in Martin's mind. His shirt stuck to his chest, glued there by Martin's sweat and Ngyuen's blood. Martin wanted to scream. He wanted to go back home to his bed where he could sleep. He just wanted to wake up the next morning. Wake up after a nightmare. A terrifying nightmare.

He passed the Saigon Notre-Dame Cathedral Basilica, illuminated by the red light of flares, and muttered a quick prayer for his own safety. Martin dived down into a side street. He hid in the darkness for a few minutes, his breathing ragged and his body shaking.

Nguyen was *dead*! He'd goddamn died for his goddamn country right in front of Martin's goddamn eyes! And Martin had captured the poor bastard's final moments on camera. He felt sick. It all felt wrong. His hands trembled and tears formed in his eyes.

This was what he had come to Vietnam for, this is what Kent wanted him to do, but taking photos of the poor bastards dying to the VC in the war just wasn't right. Martin shouldn't be here. Martin should have been back in Greensburg, Virginia, snapping photos of tour buses as they shot through the town. Not taking pictures of Vietnamese kids about to die.

"Don't move," a voice said behind him. He felt cold metal pressed against the back of his head. "VC?"

"American," Martin whispered, his voice quivering.

"Good." The voice breathed a sigh of relief and removed the weapon from Martin's neck. "Come with me."

Martin turned around and watched as the man shoved his pistol into a holster on his hip. He looked like an unremarkable man, dressed in a smart shirt with the two top buttons undone, a pair of dark slacks, shined loafers, and had a set of thin-rimmed square glasses over his beady eyes. The guy looked like a regular desk jockey. But Martin knew what type of men were sent to Vietnam. "You CIA?" he asked, trailing behind the man.

"CIA?" The man snickered. "Not that important, kid. But I do work for the government. Come on, this way." He opened a door to his left and led Martin upstairs to a cramped but insanely organised apartment. Piles of neatly filed newspapers towered above a desk. Below the skyscrapers of printing, a fan whirred away, blowing cool air across the room. "Heard you whimpering outside," he said, setting the pistol next to the fan, and grabbed a packet of cigarettes from a drawer. "Thought you were a gook or something." He offered Martin a cigarette, who accepted with a shaking hand.

"No," Martin said. "I— I was just at the palace."

"I heard the fighting from here," the man said. "It's a goddamn mess out there." He opened the door to his small balcony and the sound of war came crashing in. The man lit his cigarette and stared outside for a while.

Martin took a seat on the edge of the man's bed. After fumbling about with his own lighter, he took a deep, soothing drag from the cigarette and watched the man by the balcony.

He was taller than Martin had first thought and was incredibly skinny. His shirt hung off of him like he was a scarecrow out in a cornfield. “The name’s MacArthur,” he said, spinning around on his heels. He offered Martin his hand. “Arthur MacArthur.”

“Martin Compton.” Martin shook the man’s hand.

“Pleasure,” MacArthur said. He perked a brow and gestured to the blood on Martin’s shirt. “You been hit?”

“No, no,” Martin said, and the image of Nguyen’s head splitting open flooded his mind. He steadied himself on the edge of the bed and sucked on his cigarette. His hands began to shake a little less and he could no longer hear the thumping of his heart. Just the rattling of machine gun fire in the distance. “It’s not mine.”

MacArthur grunted. “You a reporter?”

“A photographer.”

“For what, AP?” MacArthur asked, leaning on his desk. “CBS? NBC?”

“The Greensburg Daily Herald,” Martin said.

“The what now?” MacArthur coughed. He slapped his chest a few times before taking another drag from his cigarette. “Just what the hell is a small town newspaper doing in Viet-goddamn-nam?’

Martin shrugged. “What the hell is a small town newspaper *not* doing in Vietnam?” he limply said.

MacArthur snorted. “That’s fair enough.” He looked at Martin, wrinkling his brow. “So what the hell you doing out on the streets when all this is going on? Taking photos?”

Martin bobbed his head. “Something like that, yeah”

“Well if you want my advice, stay here,” MacArthur said. “Stay here, wait it out, let the bastards who are paid to do all that fighting sort it out. Ain’t our business now, is it?”

“I suppose not,” Martin said. The night before, he’d have agreed wholeheartedly. But he just thought back to Nguyen’s resolve. The resolve that had gotten the poor kid killed.

“I mean you don’t go to a farm and pick the crops yourself, do you?” MacArthur went on. “No! You let the farmer do that. So in war, you let the soldiers sort out the fighting, the politicians sort out the politics—”

“And what do you do?”

MacArthur scowled at the interruption. “Administration,” he said. “So you let me sort out the admin of this god forsaken country and you... Take photos.” He tapped cigarette ash into an ashtray and paused as the distant cacophony of rockets and gunfire got louder. “Sounds like a damned mess out there.”

Martin shuddered and took another drag from his cigarette. “I didn’t know the VC were going to attack Saigon”, he said.

MacArthur huffed. “Neither did Saigon,” he said. “You know there was supposed to be a ceasefire for Tết, right?”

“Yeah.”

“Damned slippery commies.” MacArthur cursed under his breath. “The only way they can win a war is by breaking truces. If they win, this country’s goddamn doomed.”

Martin perked a brow. “You think they’re going to win?”

“Not at the moment.”

“We’re winning the war, then?” Martin asked.

“Sure we are”, MacArthur said. He stubbed his cigarette out and walked over to his desk. He nudged a pile of newspapers slightly to ensure they were all in line with one another. “We’ve got more numbers than they do,” he went on. “Better weapons, *more* weapons. Choppers, napalm, more bombs, more planes, ships. It’s all a numbers game, kid. Everything in this war comes down to numbers and statistics.” He offered Martin a thin-lipped smile. “We fight a battle and after it’s all done, we count the numbers. How many dead gooks, how many dead Americans. And if they've lost more than we have, then we've won. All a numbers game, see?"

Martin shook his head, thinking back to outside the Presidential Palace, back to Nguyen's corpse bleeding out on the road, his hopes and dreams for the future draining from his skull. Christ, he was just a kid. "But they're not just numbers, are they?" he asked. "They're people. Men, boys. With families and dreams, and all that."

MacArthur shrugged loosely. "That's some dangerous thinking there," he said. "You might end up on the wrong side of history thinking like that. They've signed up for it."

"But some haven't," Martin protested. "The draft and—"

"Listen, kid, I don't want to talk politics." MacArthur sighed and waved a dismissive hand. "You're clearly shaken up. Whatever you've seen, forget about it. We'll pull through. Westmoreland will send more troops and we'll overwhelm the gooks. Numbers, remember? Send in thousands of troops into the city and it'll all be over. Let's see what the radio's saying, yeah? Radio Saigon's usually interesting enough. You speak Vietnamese?"

"No."

"Bastard of a language. Don't even bother, if you

want my advice." MacArthur fiddled about with the small radio on his desk. What sounded like some sort of waltz was playing on the radio. "They're playing this shit?" MacArthur scoffed.

They continued listening to the radio for a while, expecting to hear some sort of announcement, but they only heard Viennese waltzes and traditional martial music. Eventually, the music stopped for a brief moment, but a Beatles song soon fired up soon after the pause. MacArthur rolled his eyes. "I never cared much for this album. *Revolver*, right? From '66?"

Martin smiled wide. "Yeah, it is," he said as Lennon's almost drone-like voice filled the apartment. *Tomorrow Never Knows* was a doozy.

"You like these guys?" MacArthur asked.

Martin nodded. "I got their photo when they drove through Greensburg," he said. "At least I think it was them." Kent had told Martin that he was going to print the photos regardless of whether they were The Beatles or not. Martin hoped they were.

"I think they're a bunch of goddamn commies. All you need is love, my ass." MacArthur continued to frown as the song continued to play and lit up another cigarette. Halfway through the song, the phone rang and MacArthur scrambled to answer.

"Yeah?" he asked. "Okay. Goddamn it, Jack. Really? Shit. Christ's sake. Alright, alright. Thanks for letting me know." He sighed, exasperated, and pinched the bridge of his nose. "Yeah, what a fuckin' Wednesday this'll be. Bye." He hung up and set the phone down before turning to Martin. "Bastard's have attacked the embassy," he said, without any gravitas or emotion. It was as if he was telling Martin how the weather was going to be tomorrow.

"*Our* embassy?" Martin asked, wide-eyed.

"Yeah." MacArthur sighed and perched himself on the edge of his desk. He wafted his cigarette around. "They've got balls, these gooks, I'll give 'em that. God damn typical!" He clenched a fist. "I was supposed to do a presentation this morning at the embassy. Stayed up all night working on it. The hours I've goddamn wasted. I suppose it'll have to be pushed back.."

Martin stared at him, aghast. "... The embassy's been attacked and you're worried about a presentation?"

"Yeah," MacArthur said. "I've been busting my ass trying to get it sorted."

"People are dying out there and you're annoyed that a meeting is rescheduled?"

"I've got a busy week, alright? Get off my case."

There was a cruel, distant coldness to the man's eyes which sent a shiver down Martin's spine. "You're just some photographer from some small town in where'd you say, Virginia? What the hell are you going to do about it anyway? You gonna fight the gooks at the embassy?" He erupted into laughter. "Pick up a rifle and shoot them all dead, huh? Just stay put and wait for the other bastards to do it for you. Remember kid, all about the numbers."

Martin flared his nostrils. "Come with me to the embassy," he said, surprising himself with his bold order.

"What?" MacArthur blinked. "You crazy? You outta your mind?"

"Maybe!" He sure felt crazy. Why the hell did he want to go to the embassy anyway? It was under attack. Soldiers were there. The Vietcong were there. Danger was there! So why the hell did he want to go?

He thought back to Nguyen, to the man's death, to his queer commitment to duty that Martin could never understand. Was this what it felt like, to want to help? To do one's duty? "I don't know," Martin said, mostly to himself. "Come on, we might be able to help."

"Sure, kid. You run along and get yourself shot."

MacArthur waved him away. I'm staying right here. Guess I can go through my notes again."

Martin looked at MacArthur and saw the man for what he was. A damned coward! A coward who would rather let other men, younger and better men, die so that he could live. This pencil-pushing bastard was far too removed from any of the fighting to know what it was like. Hell, Martin barely even knew what it was like but he still hated that look in MacArthur's eyes, the flippant disregard for the boys who were fighting and dying. To this man, they were just numbers, just statistics, and he didn't even want to know a thing about them! How could he just see these poor kids as numbers? They had homes to go back to, families who loved them, dreams to follow! Martin saw all the horror of war in the plain, beige face of MacArthur, the bureaucratic horror that kept wars like this goddamn one afloat.

Surely *this* is what the people of Greensburg, Virginia would want to see. The bastards running the operation who didn't care about human lives, or if they did they didn't have the decency to show it.

"You mind if I take your picture?" Martin asked, bringing his camera up.

"What the hell you want a photo of me for?" MacArthur asked.

"I just do." Martin looked through his camera's viewfinder and saw MacArthur's thin, angular, and offensively unremarkable face.

Click.

Martin nodded to himself, adjusted his camera's sling and made his way out of the apartment.

"Hey, where the hell are you going?" MacArthur called out.

"To the embassy!" Martin shouted, hoping his voice wouldn't betray the sheer terror he was feeling at the thought of actually going to the embassy. He felt like a man possessed. "To see what the hell's going on, and to see if I can help!"

"You're a fool!" MacArthur cried. "A goddamn fool!"

Martin sure felt like a fool. He didn't really know why he wanted to go to the embassy, to where the fighting was hardest. But he'd rather be a fool than a coward like MacArthur.

Dawn was beginning to break over Saigon. The lazy winter sun crawled through the smoke-stained skies, rising lethargically over the war-torn streets, firefights, and bombed-out buildings. In the cruel light of the morning, Martin saw all the chaos of the night before.

Some streets seemed untouched until you looked a little closer and you saw a bullethole in a building, dark stains on the pavement. Others looked like hell on earth. Rockets had crashed into buildings, blowing rubble onto the street. Shell casings littered the streets, bodies were propped up lifelessly against walls, helicopter blades whirred overhead, and the choking smell of smoke and cordite was thick in the air.

And hell, it wasn't even over yet. Martin could hear what seemed like a thousand and one firefights taking place in the streets, and missiles crashing through the air. But for some reason, a reason he couldn't quite understand or hope to explain, he found himself making his way to the American Embassy, despite the sounds of the fighting getting closer and closer.

As he turned down the street of the embassy, Martin saw the black helmets of the military police and a couple of marines surrounding the white walls of the compound.

One soldier dressed in an immaculately-clean uniform came rushing over to him with a big smile on his face. "*Annyeong*", he said, tipping the brim of his helmet. It hadn't been adorned with any pins, badges, or the sardonic writing that other soldiers in Vietnam had taken to doing.

"What's that?" Martin asked. "Sorry, I don't speak Vietnamese."

"Oh it ain't Vietnamese," the young soldier said.. "It's Korean."

"... Why the hell you talking to me in Korean?"

"Well I was sorta hoping you spoke it. No-one seems to speak it here."

"We're in Vietnam, Lieutenant," Martin said, noticing the soldier's insignia. "Not Korea." He frowned at the soldier who simply smiled at him. "Why the hell do you speak Korean anyway?"

"Oh I started learning it because I knew I'd be sent to Vietnam", the soldier said, the smile never fading from his round, fresh face. He was clean-shaven, though Martin doubted whether the lieutenant was even old enough to grow anything on his face, with bright blue eyes, and blonde hair poking out beneath his helmet. The man's boots shone like mirrors and he had an engraved pistol holstered on his hip.

"But they don't speak Korean in Vietnam," Martin said, his eyes narrowed.

"Oh, no. I know that."

"So why'd you learn Korean if you knew you were being sent to Vietnam?"

"I thought it was Vietnamese."

Martin blinked. "What?"

"I thought it was a Vietnamese phrase book I bought," the lieutenant said. "But it wasn't. It was Korean." He shrugged. "But my pa always told me never to start a job I don't intend to finish. So I read that book cover to cover. I reckon I'm pretty damn good at Korean now. Oh, we should probably get into cover."

Martin shook his head in disbelief and followed the lieutenant to the left of the wrought iron gate of the embassy. They both crouched behind it. Gunfire rattled from the embassy compound but in the poor light of the early morning, the soldiers surrounding the walls didn't quite know what to do but fired a few shots off anyway like the good American military training establishments had taught them.

"You're from Virginia, right?" Martin asked, the accent on the lieutenant as thick as gravy.

"Sure am, mister," the soldier said with another stupid smile. "Danville."

Martin nodded and offered his hand. "Greensburg, myself."

The soldier shook his hand. "Ain't never heard of

Greensburg but it's a pleasure to meet you, mister. Thomas Jackson— Er. *Lieutenant* Jackson, now."

"Martin Compton," Martin smiled. A bullet pinged off the cast iron fence above where the two were crouching. Jackson whooped and Martin froze.

"You a reporter, Mister Compton?" Jackon asked, eyeing the camera around Martin's neck.

"A photographer," Martin said.

"Boy, you sure came at the right time!" Jackson's smile widened as more gunshots rang out nearby, far too close for comfort. "Reckon we'll be going in soon enough. We've been firing at the gardens but it's been dark, y'see. It's somethin' alright! And to think, I weren't even 'sposed to be in Say-gone."

Martin cocked his head and looked at the fresh-faced lieutenant. He craned his neck and looked at the gaggle of MPs firing into the compound. Jackson wasn't wearing a uniform like theirs. "What do you mean?" he asked.

"Well, I just arrived in country yesterday," Jackson said. "I ain't even joined my regiment yet, but all this fightin' started and well, I just had to get stuck in! Like my pa always said, if there's a job you gotta do, you gotta do it good. So I been helping out where I can, y'see? Showing them gooks who's boss! Y'know who's boss in Saigon?"

"At the moment it looks like the VC," Martin said.

"The VC?" Jackson shook his head. "No mister, it's the USA! And we're the greatest country on God's green earth, let me tell you. We'll figure all this Vietnam stuff out for them Vietnamese. Fight the good fight!"

Martin picked at a finger, dried blood crusting behind his fingernails. Was it Nguyen's? He looked up at Jackson and felt a pang of pity in his stomach. This kid was living in a dream alright. How long before he ended up like poor Nguyen, his brains splattered across some Saigon street? This kid didn't know what the war was like. He was so pumped up full of foolish patriotism like a firework ready to burst. "You said you arrived yesterday?" Martin asked.

"Yessir." Jackson nodded. "Graduated from West Point a couple weeks ago. I ain't even seen any of them monkeys yet!"

Martin frowned. "You can't just call the Vietnamese monkeys, lieutenant."

"Not the Vietnamese!" Jackson said, exasperated. He shook his head and rolled his eyes. "I'm talking about the big apes we're fighting over here. Y'know, like in the jungle."

"The apes?"

"Yeah, the gorillas!" Jackon said. "We're here to fight the gorillas."

Martin wrinkled his forehead as he looked at the young lieutenant before realising what the hell he was on about. "You mean the VC, right?" he pinched the bridge of his nose. "The VC ain't gorillas like the monkeys. They're guerrillas. Guerrilla fighters. It's Spanish."

"The monkeys are Spanish?"

"No, the word. *Guerilla*. It's Spanish for little war."

"Then why the hell do they call them gorillas?"

"They... They don't." He looked at the Lieutenant who looked as if he was vibrating. "You alright there, Lieutenant?"

"Oh, just excited!" Jackson exclaimed.

"For what?"

"Well to attack!" He drew the pistol from his holster. "To take the embassy back from the gooks. Shoot 'em good." He took aim at an imaginary figure across the street. "Bang! Bang! Just like they taught us." He smiled again. "I'm shakin'. That normal, to shake?"

Martin looked down at his own shaking hands. He needed a damned cigarette. "I guess so."

"I feel real funny in my stomach, y'know. Like I just want to burst!"

"You're scared?" Martin asked. More gunshots from inside the embassy rang out, the frantic rat-tat-tat piercing through Martin's ears. In the distance, he heard helicopters heading towards the embassy, the rhythmic whirring of blades stirring up dust and leaves. Military police crouched down low and began to crawl along the gutters and the embassy wall. Others reloaded their weapons and got into formation.

The familiar feeling in his stomach, the fear, the terror, all came back to him. Why the hell was he still here? What the hell had Nguyen's death done to him? He should have stayed with MacArthur, where it was safe.

Jackson continued to bob up and down, excited and grinning. "No!" he said. "I ain't scared of much."

Martin frowned. "I can see that," he said and looked over the vehicle. One of the military policemen, his black helmet bobbing up and down as he moved, rushed across the street and headed towards the embassy gate. He slammed his shoulder hard against it and roared as it swung open.

Orders were frantically barked and soldiers rushed in behind him.The deafening din of M16s filled the air and grenades were hurled through the air, landing on the ground with a thud before exploding. . Inside the compound, frantic cries in Vietnamese were swiftly silenced by the crack of rifles.

"Oh shoot!" Jackson cried out. "I gotta run, can't miss this!" He drew his pistol and rushed across the street to join in the fighting.

"Hold on!" Martin called out. "I want to get your —" Jackson hurried through the open gate and was gone, lost to the fighting. "... Picture."

The sound of fighting grew louder, fiercer, and the urge to run and hide boiled up inside of Martin.

But then he thought back to MacArthur, to the cowardly desk jockey who didn't give a damn about the men on the ground fighting in this war, and who only thought about numbers and statistics. Lieutenant Jackson wasn't a number and he sure as hell weren't no statistic. He was a naive kid from Virginia who had no clue what lay in store for him in Vietnam. He'd be lucky to survive when in country. If the VC didn't get him, his men might instead, for what grizzled veteran of Vietnam would follow a boy into combat who had learnt Korean instead of Vietnamese?

The image of the bullet piercing through

Ngyuen's skull invaded Martin's mind again, and he suddenly had a desire not to let that same fate befall poor Jackson. Had Martin been the reason for Nguyen's death? If Martin hadn't asked for his photo, would Nguyen have been shot? Martin couldn't afford to think like that, but he had to see what the hell Jackson was getting himself into. This was war. Sure, it wasn't his war but Martin was here. His father couldn't think him a coward now. He was deep in the fighting in Saigon and everyone had to see what was going on in Saigon this morning. Everyone had to see the men that were fighting. The men who had died. And the men who were happy to send boys off to war.

Goddamn it but Zachary Kent was right. America really needed to see what was happening over in Vietnam so that the boys could all come home. And it was Martin's duty to get it all on camera. His duty to the States *and* to the Vietnamese, so that their country would finally know some peace.

He rushed after Jackson, his head down as he darted across the street. A helicopter hovered overhead as Martin reached the embassy gardens. He came to a halt and looked around the compound. Up ahead, soldiers jumped from the helicopter in the air, landing on the embassy roof and disappeared through a door. But aside from the shouting, it was eerily silent.

Bodies lay strewn across the green, grassy lawn. Most bodies were Vietnamese, dressed in green and brown clothes, red armbands on their sleeves, their weapons still clutched tightly in lifeless hands. There were a handful of American bodies too and Martin wandered over to them to see if he knew any of them. To his relief, Jackson wasn't among them. He counted five in total. Five boys, who had dreams, families, thoughts, and feelings, all gone. A frog, blissfully unaware of the chaos that had ended as soon as it began, hopped through blood that was pooling around the head of a dead Vietnamese fighter.

Martin bent double and retched.

A score of reporters, film crews, and other photographers began to filter through the gates of the embassy and marvelled at the chaos, filming the hole that had been blasted into the outer wall of the embassy that Martin reckoned the VC had used to get into the compound. It was a small hole, black at the edges, with the steel reinforcements of the wall all gnarled and twisted. Martin composed himself, pushed past a reporter and found Jackson, staring at the dead body of a Vietnamese boy. The fighter's lifeless eyes seemed to glisten in the dawn's sun. His tanned face was flecked with blood. He sorta looked a little like Nguyen.

Martin looked at Jackson who seemingly hadn't noticed him. "You alright, lieutenant?" he asked.

Jackson blinked and swallowed hard. His hands hung lifelessly by his side, his fingers loose around his pistol. He nodded slowly. "Yeah."

"You sure?"

Jackson clenched his jaw. "I killed him," he said.

"Yeah," Martin said. "You did."

Jackson sniffed and glanced at Martin. His eyes were narrow and wet, bloodshot and distant. It was not quite the look he'd once seen in Nguyen's weary eyes, but there was a chilling coldness, a twisted perversion in the boy's look that seemed to sum everything up for Martin. Gone were the bright blue eyes that were so full of hope, so full of wonder. It had only taken a few minutes for all that to be ripped away.

It seemed wrong but Martin had to ask. "Can I take your photo?"

Jackson's face was like stone. He simply nodded. "Sure, mister," he said, his voice cracking slightly.

Martin crouched down next to Jackson, looked

at the boy's face through the viewfinder, and pressed down on the shutter release.

Click.

"Thanks, lieutenant," he said, standing back up. Martin dusted down his trousers and gave Jackson's shoulder a reassuring squeeze. Jackson didn't react.

Martin spent the rest of the morning at the embassy, watching the reporters that had flocked there. They were all acting like an old man who watches birds on a sunny afternoon in his local park.

A soldier escorted a lone Vietnamese fighter out of the embassy building, the only survivor of the attack, and Martin eyed the weary-looking figure being led out at gunpoint. General Westmoreland arrived shortly after the fighting had stopped and ordered that things be cleared up and embassy staff return to work by midday. Martin hovered around the General as he was giving an interview for the cameras.

"General," a reporter began. "How would you assess yesterday's activities and today's? What is the enemy doing? Are these major attacks or—"

An explosion interrupted the reporter, but Westmoreland simply looked over to where the sound had come from.

"That's EOD setting off a couple of M79 duds, I

believe," he said with a calm smile. The smile seemed damned twisted to Martin. How could this man smile on a day like this? "The enemy, very deceitfully," Westmoreland went on, "has taken advantage of the Tết truce, in order to create maximum consternation within South Vietnam..."

Martin walked away from the General and out onto the streets. The sound of fighting was still there, firefights and battles raging in the distance. Martin took one more look at the embassy, at the swarm of reporters, and shook his head. He just wanted to get away.

February 4th, 1968

The fighting in Saigon didn't end when the embassy was retaken, and raged for days after. More US soldiers arrived in the city and fought to repel the VC who had taken the fight from the jungles to the streets of the capital. Martin had returned to the headquarters of the Greensburg Daily Herald in Vietnam as soon as he could, making his way through barbed wire, rubble, and piles of corpses on the streets and into the safety of the red tint of the office's darkroom. Damn it but he needed these photos developed. It was the least he could do for the poor bastards still fighting and for the poor guys who had died.

Why the hell had Martin's father ever wanted him to have enlisted? His father had been in the thick of a war, fighting an unrelenting enemy, surrounded by dead and dying friends. Martin had only been a photographer, not a soldier, but he'd seen all the horrors of war and wouldn't wish those thoughts and images on anyone.

His dreams were wracked by images of Nguyen, bleeding out on the floor and blaming Martin for getting him killed. Martin remembered how important the dead were to the Vietnamese and wondered if Nguyen's spirit would ever find peace. And so every night, Martin lit a candle and a stick of incense and offered shakily whispers of forgiveness to Nguyen, wherever he had gone. He'd even thought of going to one of the local temples and asking for advice from the monks but couldn't bring himself to. They had more important people to help.

Some days after the fighting had begun, Martin rushed back to the darkroom. He looked over his photos and slid them into an envelope, making his way to Kent's office.

"Come in!" Kent was sitting at his desk, reading

over a newspaper. He adjusted his sunglasses and looked up at Martin. "What the hell are you doing here?" he said.

"Sorry, sir," Martin said, holding the envelope behind his back. He looked behind at the empty corridors and frowned. "Where's Duc?"

Duck's dead," Kent said with a glum face. "VC killed him and his family."

Martin swallowed hard. "Poor kid," he said. He didn't want to know the death toll from the fighting over the past few days. He'd seen the body bags on the street on his way to the office, and the sounds of fighting still kept him up at night. Just how many VC were still in Saigon?

"You'll be dead in a minute, kid," Kent growled. "What the hell are you still doing in Saigon?" He slammed the newspaper down on the desk. "You should be in Khe Sanh. What happened?"

Martin steadied himself from the verbal barrage and wiped a drop of Kent's tobacco-stained spittle from his cheek. "I got caught up in the fighting, sir", he said nonchalantly.

"Got caught up in the fighting, goddamn it." Kent leant back in his chair and rubbed at his temples. The man grabbed a cigarette packet from a drawer and lit one, taking a deep drag as his eyes fixated on Martin from beneath his mirrored sunglasses. "You know how many strings I had to pull to get you on a flight to Khe Sanh? A goddamn hundred of them!" He slammed a fist down on the desk, jolting a coffee mug. Small beads of brown ran from the rim of the cup.

"I got some photos, sir," Martin said with a slight smile. That'd shut him up.

"Of what? More Vietnamese school children?"

"No, sir." Martin shook his head. "Of the fighting. The war. Just like you said, sir. Ain't no need to go to Khe Sanh when the war comes to Saigon."

Kent looked to one side and sighed. "Go on, then," he said, his voice less than enthusiastic. "Let's see." Martin slammed the envelope down on the desk and watched as Kent flicked through the three photos. "What the hell is this?" he asked, holding up the photo of Nguyen. Martin swore he could see the muzzle flash in the distance from the gun that shot the poor soldier. "A gook soldier," Kent said, flicking the photo away. He pulled out the photo of Arthur MacArthur. "Some guy in a goddamn shirt," he said. "And some tired-ass looking lieutenant?" He frowned at the photo of Lieutenant Jackson and shook his head. "What the hell's this supposed to mean?"

"The Vietnamese soldier died after the photo was taken," Martin said, grabbing the photo. "Look in his eyes, sir. He's been fighting for—"

"I don't care how long he's been goddamn fighting for!" Kent snatched the photo out of Martin's hand. "What the hell you getting photos like this for? It ain't a goddamn high school photo album out here! And this guy?" He jabbed a greasy finger onto MacArthur's rat-like face. "How long's he been fighting?"

"Oh he ain't fighting, sir," Martin said. "He works for the government. Deals in statistics. I thought he perfectly represents the politics of—"

"The people don't need anymore goddamn politics going on!" Kent took a loud sip from his coffee, letting out an obnoxious sigh of satisfaction. "God only knows there's enough of that back home." He spat to the side and held up the photo of Jackson. "And then this guy?"

"He's from Virginia, sir," Martin said. "Recently graduated from West Point. His first day in Vietnam. I met him at the embassy just before we took it back. That photo was taken after his first..." Martin blinked. "Well, his first kill, sir. "

"Why didn't you get a photo of the kill?"

Martin narrowed his eyes. He thought back to

the blood of that morning, to Nguyen's splintered skull, to the frog hopping through a pool of blood in the embassy gardens, to the stench of the bodies. Goddamn it, he wanted to forget that smell. "It didn't seem appropriate, sir."

"Compton you son of a bitch, that's what the people want!" Kent ripped off his glasses. "That's what wins awards, that's what gets played on NBC, that's what gets the people back home to wake up. Photos like this!" He held up a newspaper and pointed at a photo of what looked like an execution on the streets of Saigon. Both men were Vietnamese. One man wore a uniform, the other was dressed in a simple checked shirt. The uniformed man had fired his pistol, and the photographer had taken the photo at the very moment the trigger was pulled. It was a brutally impressive photograph.

"That's a bit graphic, sir," Martin said.

"Eddie goddamn Adams. Works for A.P. He's the lucky son of a bitch who got this on film." Kent shook his head, letting the newspaper fall onto the desk. Martin stared at the face of the man in the checked shirt, at the anguished expression as the bullet tore through his head. " Now why the hell didn't you get a photo like this?" Kent asked. "The type of photo that would have Walter goddamn Kronkite wiping away his tears on air."

"I didn't see anything like that, sir," Martin said.

"Well you better, kid." Kent said, glowering at Martin. "Else you're goddamn fired. I'll arrange transport for you to get to Khe Sanh again. Get me a photo like Eddie Adams's or I'll make the rest of your life a living hell. You got that?"

Martin sighed. "Yes, sir," he said. "Loud and clear."

"Good. Then get out of my office."

The next day, a helicopter flew Martin to an airbase outside of Saigon that was still under fire from the VC, and was loaded onto a plane and flown to Khe Sanh. He met up with Lieutenant Jackson in the middle of the fighting, but his camera stayed in his bag.

One week later, the Greensburg Daily Herald ran with the headline:

> ***Local Photographer Dead in Vietnam*** *- more on page 7.*

THE ANCIENT MARINA

CALUM DICKINSON

Her lips were turning blue again as Anthony Pageant felt his back creak, moving her still limp body. Deadlifts at the gym barely gave an inkling of beads of sweat and now it was pouring off him as he was struggling to lift the dead. His thinning hair plastering itself to his scalp, like a drowned albino rat trying to swim from a sinking ship. She had done this to him, with every crack of the camera; every flash of light, a little bit of his life was taken away.

The flash of light... the flashlight in his hand... the blood dripping from it.

The whale breaching suddenness of the strike caused his heartbeat to ripple through his veins with enough force to perceive the rocking of the boat. The smear of red on the deck of The Lamia as the photographer was squeakily dragged to the edge. The metallic smell of blood that had that sweetness about it which held stickily in his nose. No gulls cry out their accusations at him, the silence of the still sea was just as deafening though. A whisper of praise if there had been a wind to carry it hung densely in the fog. The body hitting the water releasing tiny droplets of pain as the salt stung at his cracked lips. Anthony grimacing at the pain, although not just physical but with how he had seen Marina Samodi getting younger.

Anthony's muscles flexed, pushing against his shirt as he ran through the park a few days before. His dark hair immaculate and thick, even during exertion. The cursed boat not even in his knowledge and just for a few steps more, never even seeing a dead body, let alone making one. The sleeping body on the bench should not justify his attention, let alone cause an interruption of his run, but the glint stalled him. Pacing back, Anthony pretended he was doing a cool down, as he got closer to the bench. A card holder, in the dirt covered hand, a hand that had a grey pallor of death. The face just as blue and gaunt, much like Marina's face when he would see her for the first time. He was fixated as the sun made it sparkle back at him, bewitching him. The possession of this holder was now the most important thing in the world. It would be wasted on the dead, as he took hold of it.

SNAP! went the camera on The Lamia as he felt the euphoria that he now knows was his youth being removed.

SNAP! went the finger of the homeless man as he forced the gilded card holder from the grip.

A different pleasure flowing warmth through him then, that of possession. Back when he could feel the warm blood.

Now, on The Lamia, everything made him shiver as if it was cold. Leave the dead be, the blood on his hands signaled to him that it was advice he should have heeded.

On the Lamia, Anthony's eyes were as cold and lifeless as the sinking body of Marina.

Studying his recently required loot, the glint of gold of the card holder sparked life into his eyes. The holder was immaculate, completely at odds with the rag doll he had pried it from.

Don't think of the dead... Snap went the finger... Don't think of the dead... Crack went her skull.... Think of the shine... The memories of death were replaced by the coolness under his finger tips.

The sound of the clasp opening was a gift from the gods for all the ears who heard that soft disengagement. Etched inside was Angela Fermani, a name dismissed, and clearly not the person he removed it from, as he patted himself on the back from taking it from a less deserving person. At least, it was now with someone who could appreciate the craftmanship.

There were very few things in this world that could make Anthony's jaw drop but the sight of the name on the single black card inside became one. His finger traced the embossed lettering – 'Marina Samodi'. Anthony knew that he deserved this, it was meant to be. The most eclectic and sought-after photographer in the world, now held in his hand. One folio of images would make his career, one that had passed him by, which he found rather unfair. Now, it had been handed on his lap as he burst into a giant smile. Turning over the card, in pen, was scrawled shakily "Lamia- Pier 19". Looking around, sliding the card back into the holder and concealing it, realising he needed to plot his next move.

. . .

The algae in the water at Pier 19 resembled the green concoction that he had just finished at the café, and Anthony debated on which one would be marginally tastier. The acrid smell nipping at his nose for both, that fermented smell that waved the offence under it whilst just being on the right side of festering. It may have been an affront to his tastebuds, but the vile green pond drink was a small price to pay to keep the nasty ageing process away. The first time seeing the gloopy drink, the look of surprise that appeared to only come from being struck on the head with a flashlight.

On The Lamia, Marina Samodi, the greatest photographer of this century, had stared at him, as the signal to her brain declaring "you are now dead" seemed delayed. The same way her body seemed to delay on the surface threatening not to sink, easily being able to substitute with the half submerged carcasses of the long neglected boats on Pier 19.

His back creaked like the boardwalk of the pier as he moved from the edge. His bones were on the verge of splintering like the rotting planks that had threatened to give way at each step on his way to The Lamia. His muscles twinging from the exertion of moving the body, giving that little shudder from the damp cold that surrounded him on pier 19.

The decaying remains of the other partially sunken boats looked up at Anthony, as if curious about what business he was here for. A feeling of apprehension waved through him as the mist of mystery shrouded everything around, with only the shadow of the next wreck acknowledging him, at every bowing of the boards beneath. The rhythmic thudding of one vessel that remained afloat, some form of bell clanging to a similar timing, the lapping of the wave all giving the power of the sea in motion.

The stillness of the sea now was in contrast to the moments of his attack. No pitching of the deck. Air bubbles coming straight up from Marina as she descended.

Anthony paused, ready to turn back. One rotten plank and he could go into the cold deep water. It was clear that he was in the wrong place, some form of joke played on him. A flush of red, as anger of being taken as a fool, would have become a tirade of shouts, if not for the lifting of the veil, first showing the shadow of a rather large vessel, one that danced with the ocean. His body moved forward, an uncontrolled trance, the urge to advance and seek the promise of the riches of the photography session.

The fog descended on the boat. Engulfed once more, the veil made it possible that he was on the ocean when at the pier and the pier when on the ocean. The fog of the glass had hidden Samodi's appearance as he knocked at the door. "Go away!" the figure had called to Anthony through the door.

"I should have listened" he thought as his hand trembled after his thinning blood started to slow down. The trembling hand of Samodi got steadier after every shot. The dance from behind the camera, for an old woman, was so elegant. The shapeless dress flapping as it was caught up in an artistic wind as she flowed seamlessly as a leaf in water, a sometimes-chaotic path and yet some semblance of order.

"I am here to see Marina Samodi!" Anthony called back through the thick glass of the door.

"No you are not," came the reply as the conversation pitched back to him like The Lamia in the ocean.

The anger he had then for this person... the confusion

now as he realised it was Samodi giving him a chance to leave and yet he had stayed.

All he could think about was getting by this gatekeeper, this assistant, this annoyance.

"I was recommended by a friend," Anthony blurted out as he could almost hear the click of the camera, the scream of adoration at being seen as one of the few subjects of the recluse, Samodi.

The door opened a crack to give two new windows. If eyes were the windows to the soul, then what looked back at him were triple-glazed. Glasses so thick, they must have been produced at the factory which does the bottom for glass bottles.

"Who?" called the magnified owl eyes, pupils to a monstrous proportion as they flicked back and forth. His thoughts went back to the gallery when he had first seen Samodi's work and his mind went blank.

He was at a loss, until his hand found itself on the card holder. He had not even realised it was in this pocket, but found himself stroking the engraving, once more for luck.

"Angela Fermani" as the name had blazed in his mind next to that vile green swill. There was a raising of an eyebrow, a smirk and the gatekeeper stood aside. Clearly amused and yet there was something more, a look of disappointment, a look of loss. Anthony was one step closer to Marina Samodi and yet that step was remembered to feel like an eternity as he played back going past her in his mind.

Her wiry candy floss hair bouncing back and forth in the wind as he walked past her.

Her luscious locks moved like seaweed as she sunk further, with a red misting as the head wound bled into the surrounding water.

"Where is she then?" Anthony asked as he turned to see the goldfish bowl eyes on top of a shapeless robe. Many see the old as wise, but all Anthony could see was decay, decay that he fought the impossible battle to avoid.

Her seaweed hair... The smell of seaweed drying in the air on a beach, clawing at his nostrils with the apparent sole purpose as to offend. He took a step back from the railing of the boat, breathing shallow hoping that the memory of the stench would leave him. His life was crumbling, his sandcastle of life collapsing as the tide flowed around him.

The ocean wave raised up...

Her arms raised up...

The wave tumbled down...

Her hands spread out, and she declared "She is here" with a gravelly cackle! As half the sandcastle collapsed.

She was no longer laughing; no sound was ever going to come from her again.

Anthony had to put all his distaste of the woman aside. She was the embodiment of death, the inevitable future that was to come.

"You will take my photograph then?" he asked, wondering what she could possibly want in return. "After!" She blurted out, "We must go to sea!" as she gestured out to the expansive water.

"What do you mean?" Anthony followed her wondered gaze, trying to see what was seen in the vastness.

Nothing!

Nothing was out there... He glanced at his aging eyes in the mirror, nothing was there anymore, only the abyss... And then there was a little light in his eye, and when he looked closer, it was a woman. A woman sinking down. Soon it would join the nothingness.

"I work in the ocean," she called to him "I live for the ocean" with a painful smile across her face.

And you will die for the Ocean.

Anthony's memory of hitting her on the head flashed again. A flash of the dancing, a flash of the stumbling, a flash of the fall.

The reverse of The Lamia exiting pier 19 before Marina thrust the engine forward was the roughest part of the ride. The calm of the sea as they left.

The clamminess of Anthony's skin as the shutter took the flow of life from him. He could still feel the creaking wood, moving to his weight and yet feeling solid despite the age.

There was nothing but horizon to see at the front, all he could do was look out the back of the boat as his world started to shrink in the distance. A white haze coming down made the departure all the more fleeting, quickly becoming a distant memory, like the body of Marina was starting to become as the depths swallowed her. The ocean would tell nothing about what had transpired. The waves tell no secrets, the waves tell no lies, only hides what is underneath.

Her body was still sinking, just as the boat still kept going even after the sight of land was long gone.

Further and further out to sea they went, his old life cast out and his new being reeled in.

The land was gone, the fog setting in when the tiny seeds of concern started to emerge. Anthony knew nothing about her, other than her own confirmation that she was Marina. What if she was crazy? Here he was, stuck in a boat... with nowhere to go.

"Come, come!" she said to him, tracing the path that he must follow. The studio, brighter than outside, even when it was blue sky. All white, the lightboards, which repelled all shadows from the room.

The darkness was only from within, flexing his hand with the resistance of the second skin of drying blood.

Even with the reassurance of the cameras and lenses present, it had not made him safer. Anthony would find out soon, that every time the shutter clicked, the hammer hit another nail in his coffin. A little closer to the decay that he tried to avoid.

A tired line on his forehead, a crack on his lip, a wisp of his energy mistaken as a trick of the light that headed towards Marina. She got a little stronger... She got more vibrant... She got more fluid.

• • •

Long and tiring days were par for the course when it came to modelling, the ache in Anthony's muscles seemed more lethargic than normal. He reasoned that it must have been down to the sway of the boat, having to make little adjustments to stand straight in a pose. The bandied sea legs of Marina bounced with the waves, with constant movement below the waist, and a stillness... a structure to the top half of her body. The camera steady, as if on dry land, while Anthony staggered enough that he was encouraged to sit down. His teeth gritted, as he tried to hide his annoyance at his own weakness, conjuring up more distaste for old Marina.

His distaste was enough to suck in, drying his mouth, with Marina moving faster, more fluid. The shapeless dress flapping in the artistic wind as she flowed seamlessly like a leaf on the water, sometimes chaotic and yet with some semblance of order. Marina as light as a fairy dancing on dandelions and Anthony as heavy as a candle drooping in the sun. This made it all the worse, the old having more stamina than the young. It should be him that was dancing, it should be her stuck in this chair. And yet, he could not help feel a lift inside him, something he had only felt when excited or standing up to fast. He thought it was due to the masterfulness of the Great

Samodi, little realising the light-headedness was no different to the feeling from bloodletting, as his life strings were unravelling.

The cracks on his face taunted him in the mirror, no amount of cream able to erase. The boardwalk of Pier 19, each step making the cracks deeper, each photograph making his cracks deeper. His hatred for the sea air looming like the veil of fog around him, just there... brooding. Why did he ever get on this boat? he huffed. The boat, unrocked by the waves that had met the steps of the dance with the camera. The dead calm that spread across the ocean, as he felt the hum of aches in his bones. No creak as the ship settled, as his fingers trembled from even the simple movement of touching his face. The skies empty of birds, the fish nowhere to be seen, not even some seaweed bobbing along. Nothing but fog and water. The curtain that clouded Anthony's eyes, next to land, in the middle of the ocean, he could be either. Empty and yet still feeling the vastness, his thrum of heart beating. The ever expansive and still he could feel the claustrophobia setting in.

His eyes were sunken, his skin was sallow, and his hair seemed to be getting thinner. Anthony spluttered into the sink as he wheezed.

The engine wheezed in the same way as the starter motor failed to catch to allow him to head back to land.

The weakness was all encompassing, even breathing was a task as he whimpered out “What is happening to me?”

He staggered from his cabin, getting to Samodi being the only thing driving him forward. He tried to grab her, but his legs were jelly, the table had to do as he held it for support. “What have you done to me?” he croaked.

Her lips were pink now, her skin smooth and the eyes, her soul, no longer hidden behind the glasses. She smiled at him, “It is all part of the process.” There was something behind her eyes, she spoke the words as if from a script, from a memory, a look of sadness behind the smile.

“In order for you to give everything, you must lose everything.” A hesitation. “You will have your youth returned to you at the end of the last session”. Hardly noticeable but it was there, that brief little pause.

Was she lying to him? She had to be playing him for a fool. Maybe it was drugs as he started to think what she had given him to eat. Or maybe he was hallucinating from dehydration being out at sea without any fresh water. Anthony's mind had raced through different possibilities, all avoiding the bizarre truth of the matter that Samodi was stealing his life force.

"Turn back now!" Anthony demanded. If he was back on land, everything would be solved and he could get away from this madness.

"If you interrupt the process, you will stay like this." The tone was pleading, as Samodi responded. It was clear she wanted him to stay.

Anthony was powerless, he hated not being in control and as the weakness took hold of him, there was nothing he could do.

"Let me take control" called the voice as he tried to suppress his anger. "I will get you through this".

No! He had to stay focussed, keep his wits, and he may still get out of this. He just needed a means of escape.

"Don't ignore me!" reprimanded the voice, "Think of how jealous everyone will be when you return triumphant!" The flash of the awestruck faces as he adorned the walls of an art gallery.

"Show me the photos." He shook his head as if that would somehow remove the voice. It would be worth it in the end, he told himself. This is what he wanted.

The tear did not roll down his cheek, instead along a newly formed wrinkle. His fingers tracing the bead and tracing the wrinkle. The lump in his throat as the awe from each photo shown built the emotion. Samodi was a true master, Anthony could not deny this. How she could manage to capture his pain and suffering, his struggle, and yet capturing a softer side to himself he had never seen. The next session would manage to capture a darker side, with the fog having descended around the Lamia as the sense of the foreboding started to increase.

The sea became calmer as the undercurrents took the body. The chill to the bones even without a whisper of the wind. Only the voice murmuring away, directing him, nagging him.

He could see everything in the photographs but there was nothing visible. There was no reason that these photos should fill him with such emotion.

And now he was here, strangled by the fog and stranded by the sea.

He could see nothing from her dance, how her fingers caressed the buttons on the camera. Nothing from her steering as she had started the boat. It was a dark art, both image and navigation of the sea. A simple click of the shutter, a simple turn of the key. Neither did anything without the right person being captain. Marina may have now fully sunk, but she taunted him now. The photographs in his hand, allowing for one final moment of glory.

The beauty seen in the photograph refreshed his enthusiasm for the sessions. Anthony could push aside his aches for the short session, the breathlessness, now sitting without question. He would possess Samodi's originals after this, and with that, endless opportunities everywhere. Marina was no longer taking his life, she was giving a future, a future full of riches for a little discomfort now. Her hair getting less grey, her cheeks getting plumper and rosier accenting her dimples as the camera shuttered clicked. His skin sagged and tightened in equal measure at different places. Her back straightened, no longer hunched over as if coveting, her legs wobble less as her feet danced the photographer's jig.

It was all going to be okay, Anthony told himself

as the voice sounded like it was clapping in glee as he gave himself over to the process.

"No More!" Anthony could barely gasp as he called for the session to a close.

"No More!" cried out Marina from the other room that night, waking Anthony. Stuck in the realm of awake and sleep, his tired body lay there unable and unwilling to move. No other voice responded to her, and he wondered if this was just a dream itself.

"This is the last time!" She said moment later, and with hearing it in reality, his alertness rose. The lack of bars on his phone meant they were too far out to sea. "I will not be party to the death of anyone else!".

Anthony's brain called at his legs to get up, but they were frozen. A satellite phone! He had to get hold of it, and call for help. She had lied to him.

"She is stealing your life force" told the voice, no longer telling him to carry on. "You must save yourself before it is too late!" He would give almost anything for fame and fortune, but his life was not one of them.

. . .

Breathless!

Like the last breath of Marina, so did it feel like the last breath of Anthony.

And yet, each time the camera clicked, it felt like one further gasp was exhaled, a little more air to be expelled and with it, the tendrils of his life energy made the journey over to Marina.

"She is going to kill you", Anthony felt like he should snap back at the voice that he was well aware of his predicament.

His mind was ambling, unable to think fast enough as the fog held tightly around him. The reflection of himself in the lens looked back. What had she done to his body? He could not carry on like this. He had to put a stop to this! His eyes fell on the flashlight, standing on end like a monolith.

Now here he was stuck in the ocean. He should never have picked it up. He should never have listened.

The silence in the boat only made the rasping of his breath more deafening. The sea, now devoid of movement, was enough to drive him to the brink of madness. He wandered the deck alone, the voice gone. It appeared satiated after he had killed Marina. On the deck, lay the camera. Untouched by blood, unharmed from the fall, the final captures given no indication of the violence in between. The photos were still beautiful, but at what cost. The notion that removing Marina would somehow restore his youth. Now, without the goading, without the threat of the last of his life being taken from him, the remorse and self-pity started to kick in.

"Take it!" the voice told him,

"Strike her!"

"It is the only way you can get your youth back" as Anthony stared at the flashlight.

"It is the only way you can get your youth back" as Anthony stared at the camera.

If it had worked for Marina, then could it work for him?

His knuckles were white around the instrument of her death, The Lamia boards making no sound as if in on the conspiracy. The flashlight to the sky, the swing to the ground, the shock travelling up his arm as it connected. All down to gravity, as he did not have the strength. She staggered. She turned. A look of surprise. A pinch of confusion. Hand reaching out, grasping at nothing. Dimples disappearing as her face dropped. Her mouth moving as if trying to recite an unspoken poem. Then a calm, a contentment in her eyes, a relief that something was over.

What was over for Marina was only beginning for Anthony.

Anthony's hand took hold of the camera, it felt good in his hand. An apparent match, designed as if it was always meant to be. He could use this, use it so that he could have his life returned to him. "Good" called the voice, "now start the engine".

The engine spluttered into life as he turned the key this time, the fog lifting, beckoning him as it showed him a path, making out the tiniest speck of land in the distance. He was leaving Marina behind now, the unseen buried at sea. The fiery pain that would spasm across his back tremoring that it was far from over. He still had to get his life back and then he would get off this boat and never look at it again.

The shutter clicked and he could feel it, the life force coming to him.

The unseen fog, the invisible barrier that stopped him from disembarking at Pier 19. The Lamia had guided him back, as the boat bumped on the edge of the pier making Anthony sway uneasily on his feet. The boat drove everything and now it was keeping him on board. Here he was, stuck now at the pier, with nowhere else to go. Staying spelled death, and heading back to sea would sign his fate. The footsteps along the boardwalk made him freeze, a tall shadow coming through the fog, emerging. "Are you Marina Samodi?"

"Yes, I am." Anthony replied. He could taste it, the desire of taking the photographs just now.

"Not yet!" said the voice. The call of the ocean was there. How could he go back out to sea so soon? And yet, it was the desperate need to get his life back that drove him.

The aging model that stood before him had come aboard with such hopes and dreams, completely unaware of what had befallen them. The Lamia called out to Anthony, driving him forward at transferring the energy. He could feel the life surge through him, the tingles, the warmth, redness returning to his cheeks. The pit in his stomach as he saw the model's transformation before him.

"Only take a little," thought Anthony. A little from this one, a little from the next. Or so he thought. The Lamia laughed knowing the enticement of the power, as his hunger increased. The sweet and yet acrid smell of the life force tickled his nose, as his whole body puffed up with exhilaration. The hum of The Lamia started to reverberate more, it too feeding on the energy. His hairs started to stand on his arms, electrified. His muscles started to become defined once more. His aches, on parts of his body that he never knew could have pain, dissipated. The cold fog no longer able to penetrate life's glow. The last of the life energy caused the model to disappear with a whisper. Eyes clouding over, turning lifeless. The husk, joining Marina at the bottom of the ocean.

The barrier would keep him on The Lamia, ensuring that he could not escape, and starve the boat. Tied to The Lamia permanently, the lives forever entwined waiting for the next hapless model that was willing to find him for fame. He was now Samodi, the greatest photographer in the world.

The album popped out at the end of the bed when Anthony accidentally kicked it. No jarring pain, as his youthful body was once again restored. "Portfolio shots of Angela Fermani," he read aloud as he took it up in his hands. Raising an eyebrow, this was the owner of the card holder, she was the one that started it all. He would never have found The Lamia if it was not for her. He stared dumbfounded at the woman that stared back, those dimples, they were unmistakable. She stared back at him, just as she had stared back at him as she sunk to the depths. This time there was life and a twinkle in the eyes. The look of peace was the same that she had given after he had struck her. Had she been tormented so much by this burden? If this was Angela, then who was Marina Samodi? The camera feeling like a millstone around his neck as the enormity of the situation now pressed down on him. The voicc, the Lamia, laughed at him as he came to the realisation. The Lamia was Samodi, a Venus fly trap consuming all that came aboard.

TIMELINE

EMILY SIGGERS

Ash. Rotten wood. Stale air. The faint smell of metal.

These were the first things that I noticed when I awoke. My mind tried to connect the dots, tried to link the smells, but I soon realised I had no idea. No memory. Not even my name.

I slowly opened my eyes and found that I was lying face down on wooden boards. I could feel the ridges from the wood imprinted on my face, so I knew that I had been lying there for some time. As I looked around, it became apparent that I was in an attic. A single window shone above me, although nothing interrupted the clear blue sky.

I heaved myself up from the floor, but my fingers touched something smooth instead, slipping.

Looking down, I found that my head was surrounded by photographs, all glossy but faded. The photograph that my hand had slipped on was now ripped into pieces.

I positioned my hands in between the photos, and with effort, I pushed myself up to a seated position. I was in a large room with wooden boards covering every surface. Rafters held up the sloped walls, with bright fairy lights in a chain wrapped around them. There was a small switch by my head, which when pressed, the lights dimmed, and a blind closed across the skylight, enveloping the room in darkness. Empty boxes were piled around, towards the sides of the room. Cardboard loomed around, casting claustrophobic shadows everywhere. There was a small clock on the wall, reading midday.

In the corner, there was a trapdoor.

A way out.

I raced over to the trapdoor, looking fervently for a handle or way to open the door. I found none: the only difference between it and the wood of the floor was the gold frame highlighting the only hope that I could escape this place.

Trapped.

How, how did I get here? Why was I trapped here? Where was I? Why could I not remember?

These questions and many more flitted through my mind. I sat there for what felt like hours trying to think of some answers, occasionally looking back at the trapdoor to see if it magically opened. I wracked my brain, but it was blank.

Slowly I returned back to myself and a sense of determination came over me. I needed to get out of here; at least figure out *why* I was there.

I looked at the trapdoor once again and studied it further, trying to gleam some more clues. The wood was similar to the floor, looking almost new. Moving closer, I saw scratches and bumps in the surface, spreading from corner to corner; almost like someone had tried to open it before and failed. There were tiny marks of red in between the grain, with a smell of iron emanating from it when I inhaled. Blood?

I pushed on the door , trying to see if these had affected the strength at all, but it seemed to be reinforced with something sturdier for just that purpose.

With the trapdoor a dead end, I turned to the rest of the room. The walls, except for the fairy lights, were unremarkable, and there were no gaps between the slats. The skylight was lined with gold metal, but no matter which angle I tried to look through, it still showed the same uninterrupted blue sky that I had noticed when I first woke up.

On the floor, there were many photographs strewn across the room, along with a damp mark in the shape of a body where I had laid - likely where I had sweat during my sleep. There were large shards of glass in the corner, all different shapes and sizes.

Moving towards the glass pieces, I realised they were of a broken mirror. I picked up one of the larger shards, holding it up to the light coming from the window above me.

A reflection stared back at me; a young woman, with bronzed skin, dark brown eyes and long blonde hair. She looked questioningly back at me, as if to say "Who is this?"

I looked behind me with a start, hope rising in me quickly and fading just as fast when I saw that I was still alone.

I raised an eyebrow. She raised an eyebrow. I winked. She winked.

This was me. How was the recognition not immediate?

I was wearing a faded lavender dress, which was spotted with red; blood splatters? My arms were half covered with a denim jacket, but the sleeves were fastened with buttons along them, as if the arms needed to be accessed at other times.

Her face was marked down the length of her cheek with a bright red line, caked with dried blood. My face. My cheek. One eye was black and swollen, and dried tears stained through makeup on my cheeks. Closing the other eye, I realised that my vision was obscured slightly from the inflammation. Grease coated my scalp and my hair looked filthy. It seems that I have been here for a while.

I wrenched my eyes from the mirror and looked down at my body. Bruises, cuts, scratches. And dozens, no, *hundreds*, of tiny dots scattered all over my arms and legs. Like tiny pinpricks, like I had been stabbed over and over with sewing needles or pins. By some of them, there were long tracks of red marks, like a longer needle had been used.

An injection site?

Studying my body more, I found a small tattoo on my left ankle. It was a small faded butterfly, with the words 'Fly Free' scrawled next to it. The lines were scratchy, wobbled and broke in some places, almost like it had been done by an amateur or a bad tattoo artist. The skin was not sore when I ran my finger over the top of it, and the ink moved smoothly when I pulled at it, so it was evident that it had been there for some time. The butterfly almost seemed to jump out of my skin, the antennae like eyes. "I've been here for a while." it would taunt, "Just like you."

There was one more thing to investigate: the photographs. There were dozens around, but most were faded beyond recognition, defaced with scratches, or blank white frames where a picture was waiting to be displayed. A few were blurry, but all I could see were fuzzy figures of differing heights, not even their smiles remaining on their faces.

I shuffled through the stack and sorted them, finding five or six that I could potentially get some information from. The first photo was of a small blonde haired child. She looked five or six, with a plastic tiara on and a princess dress. She held a plastic fairy wand, star on the end, and stood in front of a bright fuschia bouncy castle, smiling a toothy grin to the camera. There was a large banner strung over the top, with the words 'Happy Birthday Lena!' in large bubbled letters. Was this me? Was I...Lena?

The name didn't seem like it fit at first. I spoke the name over and over in my head and aloud, and it slowly started to feel like mine.

Photo number two had the same child, but a

little older. She was paler, thinner and looked tired. She was propped up with countless pillows in a princess themed bed, with a tray in front of her. Still smiling. The plastic fairy wand - which I recognised from the last picture - was displayed on the wall above the bed, along with the first photograph that I had looked at here. It obviously had come from her bedroom. The tray in front of her had the start of a drawing on, and she was holding a couple of crayons between her fingers.

The third photo was in a hospital bed. There was a girl there with an oxygen mask on, wired up. You could not see who it was in the mask, but there was a man standing next to her dabbing her forehead with a cloth. He was thin, athletic with short blonde hair and a worried look on his face. Was this his daughter? Get-well-soon cards were covering every possible surface, in various states of disrepair. Some were tattered and barely showing text anymore, but some could have looked brand new. Wires seemed to be coming from every place on her body and monitors hooked up to each. I couldn't tell what they read, but there were a mix of green and red symbols there.

The fourth photo I recognised as the girl I had seen in the mirror pieces just a few minutes ago. Me.

I was younger, more like a teenager. I was in a wheelchair wearing a cast on one arm. I was smiling, but something in my eyes showed something else. Exhaustion? Pain? Fear? I looked sick, thin and pale, apart from the purple and green of bruises that I could see poking out from underneath the bottom of my jeans.

I looked down at my body in disbelief, turning my legs over and around to see if they worked. There seemed to be no problem that I could see with how they worked, except for the marks covering them.

The fifth and final photograph; I was around the same age as before, but looked very different. A healthy glow was back, although I still looked slim, and the smile on my face seemed genuine. A man stood next to me holding my waist, supporting me. The man looked similar to the man in the hospital, but with slightly more refined features - his hair was buzzed and his face was slimmer. I felt a small smile upon my lips and I seemed warmed at the thought of him; something about him triggered a familiar memory that I could not bring up into my mind.

I sat back, processing everything. Emotions flooded my head, though I was not sure if it was anger, sadness or despair. Was I ill? I didn't feel ill.

Once again, I got up and stretched, trying to

focus on one body part at a time. Apart from the soreness around the cuts and bruises on my limbs, I felt...fine. I took another glance in the mirror shards and I looked like a healthy young woman. Beneath the dirt and bruises, my bronzed skin had colour in it and I was no longer sickly thin. What had happened to me?

I couldn't connect the dots yet. I knew there was something I was missing. There had to be a reason that I was trapped here, and these photographs seemed to hold the answers that I was seeking. Not like I had anything better to do than look at pictures, after all.

Hours passed by. Looking out the window now showed a quickly darkening sky, stars beginning to twinkle at me tauntingly. It was almost as if they were mocking me.

"Ha ha!" they'd say, "Come and join us if you can". Or maybe they would be sympathetic. "Oh dear child, how can we help?".

The light from the fairy lights seemed to shine brighter in the night, but it still wasn't enough to see very well. I tried scrutinising the pictures again for a while, but could not see anything with the dim light. I put the five clear pictures in a neat pile to the side, making sure that I wouldn't ruin or knock them in my sleep. I turned the switch to dim the lights, lying down in a similar place to where I woke up.

Thoughts circled in my mind, the same questions were still there than before. I had some more details to think about:

Lena was likely my name, and I am ill. Or was.

Someone must have put me here, or else I trapped myself with photographs to remember.

It also left me with a lot more questions. I was free at one time, that was evident from the photos. But how did I come to be here? Was I a danger to someone outside of this place? Was there even a place outside of here to go to?

Perhaps there was a nuclear apocalypse, and I had the only surviving cure. I couldn't smell any radiation anywhere on my body, if that was even a thing.

Was the man in the final photograph my husband? A man who had trapped me in this attic, like Mr Rochester trapping his wife in *Jane Eyre*. A book that I somehow remembered but had no memory of actually reading.

Why didn't I remember anything else?

The same thoughts circled as I struggled to fall

asleep, but eventually the tiredness took over and I fell into a deep sleep.

I was awoken by a loud clunk coming from the corner of the room, the side closest to the trapdoor. I sat up quickly and switched on the fairy lights, the stars in the night now clearly shining through the skylight.

A small plate of food had appeared next to the trapdoor, on a small porcelain plate, joined by a bigger bowl obscuring something behind it. I jumped up and ran over to the door, looking to see if there was anything different about it. It looked the same, though some more dust around it had been disturbed.

It had been opened by someone. I hadn't trapped myself here, someone else had.

I began to hammer my fists onto the door, screaming as loud as I was able. My voice sounded hoarse, like it hadn't been used or had been blown out by screaming.

"Let me out!"

No matter how much I screamed, there was no response from below. I was alone.

After my voice was all but gone and my fists

were bloodied, I sat back, defeated. The plate of food was next to me, still steaming from heat. A tiny bowl of cereal, a cooked potato topped with green vegetables and a small pile of cooked bacon. Now that I was closer, I also noticed two bottles of clear liquid were next to the plate.

So I was being fed by someone. Not that I had an appetite.

It was still night, and I wasn't getting out any time soon, so I took the food and drinks to the space I had cleared for myself to sleep. It took some time to settle myself, but I once again drifted off to sleep.

The next time I woke, it was daylight. Morning birds were calling from outside the window, and one landed on the skylight for a brief moment. It seemed to try to break in with its beak, almost like it was trying to help me escape. I watched it ruffle its feathers, leaving one floating on the glass before it flew away. The momentary contrast to the normally clear view was a welcome sight, and it helped to refresh my motivation for the new day.

Even if I didn't get out today, I was sure going to figure out what had happened to me.

The plate with food was still next to me, though

the food was no longer steaming. I took a bite from the cereal bowl to test, and it didn't *seem* like it was tainted in any way. I ate as much as I was able, which wasn't much, and left the remainder to the side for later. I drank some of the clear liquid, the sweet taste causing my lips to pucker for a moment in surprise, and set the other and remainder to the side.

I turned my attention back to the photos. These would hopefully have some more answers to what happened. I decided to lay them out in front of me in order, looking at the youngest to the oldest. Were these all me? I had a scar on my chin in both the younger ones, which matched the ones that I could see in the reflection of the mirror shards.

The hospital one was a little more difficult to confirm - I looked closely at the girl in the bed and found it difficult to see much of her without wires and the mask. Eventually, I looked at her legs and saw a small, almost missable bean shaped scar on her knee, which matched one on mine.

I studied the photograph, looking closely at the man standing next to me wiping my forehead. He still didn't feel familiar to me, and I felt a sense of dread when I looked at him, in contrast to when I looked at the younger man in one of the other photographs. My stomach turned and I felt the urge to vomit, which I was able to push down and continue.

I turned over the photograph and found a small signature in the corner that I had missed before.

‘Lena and Daddy’

So this was my father. How could I not remember him? I scanned his face, and I felt sick to my stomach.

Beeps and machine sounds are everywhere. I can’t breathe. I can’t see. What is happening?

Father wipes my brow. Plastic mask over my face and a cold breeze floats across my lips. It helps me breathe, I remember the nurse saying.

I open my eyes, I am in a hospital bed. Need to move, can’t move; too many wires.

“Lena, you need to rest” Father says, “You’re very hurt”.

‘I don’t feel hurt’, I think. Cloth feels nice on my forehead.

The nurse comes in. “We need to take you for some tests, Melanie.”

I hear Father begin to reassure me, I close my eyes and let myself drift off.

. . .

I shook all my limbs, feeling the wires covering every inch of my skin as the flashback faded. Stretching it, the needles feeling like they were going to tear before the nurse stopped me.

Melanie. So Lena was a nickname?

I put the photo to the side; that didn't seem to have any extra information. At least at the moment.

Taking the first photograph - the one with the small child on it, I looked at it a bit more thoroughly. The only child in the frame was me, in the centre, but there were a few tables behind the house that had food for a party laid out. There were a couple of adults sitting and standing around, obviously in the middle of telling a joke, as the woman sitting down had her head thrown back in laughter. The woman standing up was smiling, while serving food on the long table. She looked like the double of me now, it was like looking once again to those mirror shards.

Mama.

The word came to me without thinking. I felt an ache in my chest as I looked at her, longing as if I had lost her a long time ago. Tears came to my eyes, falling uninterrupted as I stared, breaking my view before I swept them away.

In the background of where my mother and the other woman were standing, was a house, a small thatched cottage. At first look, it looked like an idyllic country house, reminiscent of a fairy tale. Low ceilings so you would have to dip your head to walk around, the roof that looked pretty but gave out a musky smell whenever it rained. There were holes in between the thatch, sharp sticks of unwoven straw poking out the top. The walls looked fragile, like they would collapse with a wrong word or a breath in the wrong way.

An important detail to note was that there didn't seem to be an attic or skylight of any kind - this wasn't where I was now. Maybe this is where I lived with my parents? I still continued to be surprised that I had so little memories of my childhood and the time before this attic.

I felt around my head to see if I could find any bumps, bruises or cuts, like I found on my body, thinking that it could be a possible answer to why I couldn't remember anything. There was slight swelling in my eye, as though I had fallen hard on something. Looking again in the mirror shards, I could see purple stained blotches surrounding my eye. But nothing that sparked any memories. Not the answer there.

Could it be from this mystery illness that I seemed to be getting worse from in the pictures? But even then, the one memory I had from the hospital bed, I didn't *feel* ill. I was in pain from the wires, but nothing felt like it was wrong inside.

The next picture was where I was once again in a bed. I was a bit older than the first one, but this was likely before the hospital bed photograph,

The pink fairy wand from the first picture was on the wall, as I had seen before, but looking closer, it was cracked in a few places and the sticker on the star was mostly washed away, with the faded pink showing in a few broken places. I hadn't noticed before, but the first picture was displayed on the wall next to the wand, so it must have been taken from there to come into the attic with me.

The girl - I mean - *I* - was sitting up in bed, covered with a bright pink bedspread. Now that I was taking longer to look, I could see that there were a few of those wires attached to the small hand that rested on the top, clutching the crayons. On the tray below her, there was a drawing. I didn't pay much attention to it before as it seemed like a pointless child's drawing, but now I was going to take all the clues that I could get.

Rotating the picture, I tried to look closer at it. It

was difficult due to the angle and the age of the photograph - both made it blurry - but it looked like a house, with a girl in a pink princess dress standing beside. There was a taller stick figure next to her, which was waving a magic wand over the house.

I remembered this - how? I could bring the memory to my head as easily as I could remember what happened a few minutes ago.

I drew this to make my mother feel better after I was first ill. I couldn't get out of bed, so the cannula inserted in my hand was to administer fluids and medicine to help me feel better. The drawing was of our house - the run-down cottage falling apart at the seams - and my mother waving a magic wand over everything. Healing me, fixing the house. Stopping my parents from arguing.

The opposite of reality. I remembered my mother's tortured eyes everytime she looked at me in that bed - I was stuck there for weeks. Just stuck in a curtained room, separate from the outside world.

Just like where I was now, trapped with no sign of escape. Not that I knew it then.

My memory failed itself after trying to remember past that time trapped in bed. I didn't remember leaving it, or how I went from that bed to another bed in the hospital. Where had my mother gone? I suddenly felt tearful once again, the feeling of grief one again tightening my chest and crushing my heart.

I ate a little more of the plate of food from the morning, my appetite starting to come back a little. I inspected my hands as I did, and was able to find the points where the cannula would have been. There were bruises where it would have been removed, which were so bold it was almost as if they were painted on. There were scars on my knuckles, faint pink where the skin seemed to have been split repeatedly and healed incorrectly. There was a fresh mark on one, a bright red scrape shining across the bumps on my hand.

I put the two pictures together with the other for the time being. They may hold extra information that I haven't seen, but not for now.

I glanced at the fourth picture but decided to avoid it for now - something about the look in my eyes in the wheelchair was too haunting to see at the moment, my stomach fluttering with butterflies and turning over with anxiety. It would be the hardest one to look closely at, and I wasn't sure if I was ready to relive any memories from that time.

I instead looked at the picture of the other man and I, the only older one where I was standing up.

An adult now; I looked drained but happier. There was something in my eyes that showed some of the troubles that I had been through, but I looked like a happy young woman at first glance.

I could tell there was some weakness in my legs, as the man next to me was holding me up by the waist. In the background, I could faintly see a wheelchair, which matched the one in the other picture. I looked thin still, but had a healthy glow about myself as well. Perhaps the treatments I'd undergone were working?

I looked closer at the man that was holding me up. As I'd noticed before, he looked similar to the man that was mopping my forehead in the hospital. I held both pictures side by side - they were very obviously related to each other. The younger man had his hair cut short and he held himself proudly. He was beaming at the camera, seemingly pulling me closer every opportunity he could.

Jacob. The name came to me quickly, after I'd studied his face a little more. My older brother. How could I have forgotten him as well?

I remembered when this picture was taken. My father taking the picture, but glaring at me from behind the lens. He was angry, Jacob wasn't meant to be taking me out of the chair at all.

"Her legs are too weak", he'd say, "you'll do damage."

But Jacob ignored him - he wanted a picture with his sister, and to look as normal as possible. Like it was before. Jacob was there in the hospital when that picture was taken, taking the picture as my father and the nurses rushed around me.

He was in the army - he joined up when I was ten, just when I started to get ill. It made it so he was so rarely home, this picture was one of the very few times that he did as an adult. It was my eighteenth birthday, and all I wanted was to see him. He managed to get leave to come back for the week, just so we could celebrate together.

He took me out in my wheelchair to the arcade: it was the only trip out that I had been allowed with him since my illness. We didn't win anything, but spent all our change trying to get a small pink jellyfish toy out of a claw machine. I remembered feeling sad when he left, but I didn't know when that was. I smiled fondly at the memory, feeling those happy feelings once again, but they soon turned to sour dread as I remembered his abandonment of me.

Where was he now? Why had he allowed me to be trapped in this place? Did he not think about what situation he was leaving me in? I threw the picture across the room in anger, nausea and revulsion flooding my body.

I sat for a while and thought back to everything. Why now, could I remember some things, like my brother, and not others, like why I was here? It seemed to be that my mind had put up barriers around the answers that I required, taunting me like they were pushing up against the glass making faces. I knew they were there, but try as I might, they would not pull further forward.

There was one final photograph to look over. The one that turned my stomach, with that desperate look into the camera. I spent some more time looking through the empty cardboard boxes, tidying the photographs and eating food to stall, but I knew that eventually I would have to relent. It could hold more clues as to why and where I was where I was.

This photograph seemed to place me in age in the middle of the photographs, but I was in a different house than before.

This house looked very different to the original thatched cottage. It was much more modern, with tall white walls covered in brick cladding in pale white. There was a glass conservatory facing the side, which had a few wood woven sofa chairs in. I could see stacks of boxes at every square inch of space, overflowing onto one of the sofa chairs. On the side was a logo for what looked to be a syringe and a doctor's bag. Were these medical supplies?

Putting off looking at myself for now, I looked more at the house in the background. There were two floors above the ground floor, one floor that may have contained bedrooms and a boxy half attic room. Most notably, the attic room had a skylight, lined with gold metal.

The house itself seemed familiar to me, and I looked up. At the skylight, lined with gold metal.

At least one question was answered - this seemed to be where I was.

There seemed to be no further clues in the house, so I turned my attention to the part that I was dreading, my stomach tying itself into knots. I sat in the wheelchair, staring emptily back at the camera, a forced smile on my face. I looked like I was in pain, exhausted from years of suffering. My eyes were surrounded with dark circles, with a level of tiredness that only someone who had been through hell knew. My hair was greasy and unkempt, wrapped up in a loose bun. How soon was this after the previous picture, where I lay in my hospital bed?

I had a bright pink cast of my arm, held up by a

thin piece of fabric tied around my neck. I felt my arm to see if I could feel any break or scar, and I felt what seemed like a metal plate under my skin, across my forearm, exactly where the cast had been.

A long, almost invisible, scar ran down the length, with marks at points where staples seemed to have been used to hold my skin together as it healed. It seemed like an old injury, so that gave some clues as to how old I was now.

Studying myself more, I saw, again, the multi-coloured bruises on my legs. They seemed to be from removed tubes and needles, the same lines and tracks that I had seen on my hand. The hospital didn't seem to be an isolated incident; instead it was one of many times that I was there, testing and treating this mystery illness. Was the trauma of these illnesses the reason for my memory loss?

Flashes of blood tests, injections, tablets; they started rushing through my mind. Some given by the hospital, some given by my father. Some I took myself. Images upon images came up, overwhelming my senses. A blue tablet twice a day before food. A long white pill to take three times a day during meal time. Being forced injections into the backs of my arms. Spitting out a black and white pill in my father's face, and being forced to take it anyway, his hands down my throat.

I lay back on the hardwood floor, looking up at the skylight. Like yesterday, it shone uninterrupted bright sunlight into the room, hurting them if I looked too long. My eyes began to burn but I ignored it, wanting to feel something different to the despair I felt at being trapped. I ignored the feeling for as long as I could manage until I had to look away, leaving my vision blurred with sun spots and tears. When my vision cleared again and I wiped my eyes, I noticed something that I hadn't seen before.

Another photograph.

I pushed myself to my feet and walked over to the picture. It was partially covered with the undecipherable photographs from earlier in the day. It was ripped, and I realised that this must be part of the photograph that I had slipped on when I first woke up.

The picture was dim and partially faded; part of the reason that I did not see it in the first place. Holding it up to the light from the skylight, I could see a figure in a mirror. It was me.

I did not recognise the room in the background, though it was nearly completely black and blurry. I stood in front of a mirror and had a mobile phone pointing at it, my face looking down at the screen.

The bottom half of the picture was ripped, though I seemed to be standing with no problem or support. There were photographs all around the rim of the frame, many that matched the photographs I had been looking at in the attic. In the background, I saw a scrap of paper, with a pen resting on top.

As I craned to see what the letter said, a sense of dread entered my stomach, acid reflux starting to fill my throat. I sat back, and remembered.

"Lena!"

The shout upstairs times exactly with the flash on my mobile phone camera. I check it and send it quickly to my small wireless photo printer. I swiftly hid the photo from view; it was not one that my father would approve of. I cover the letter I was writing with a book, as that was the best way to hide its contents.

I move back into my wheelchair and pull a book off the low shelf to feign reading it. I focus on my breathing. Breathe in, breathe out. Zen, I try to relax. My skin feels cold, goosebumps on my arms from fear. I try not to think of the alternative, what could happen if he suspects anything. Send for more bogus tests, that's for sure.

A few minutes later, he comes into the room, with an angry look on his face. As soon as he sees me with my nose in the book, his expression softens.

"Lena, I've been calling you!" he says.

"Sorry, Father, I've been a bit occupied," I reply, holding up the book.

He walks and sits next to me on the space on my bed, which is the closest thing to eye level in the room from my space in the wheelchair.

"You're still in your wheelchair?" he asks, wiping down the bedspread next to him, as if to invite me up. "Wouldn't you be more comfortable in bed, or in your chair?"

I pause whilst I tried to think of an excuse - he knows that the wheelchair wasn't the most comfortable seat, but he also doesn't know that I knew that I could easily transfer from place to place - that was usually 'his job'.

"I didn't want to call you for something small, you seemed busy," I say, trying to act confidently. He seems to buy it, at least for the time being.

"Makeup?" he asked, flicking through one of the books I had piled around my desk, though thankfully not the one covering the letter, "Not something you normally wear in the house."

"Yeah," I hesitated; I was normally only allowed to wear it out, to disguise the grey pallor that I had constantly, "Just felt like it today."

"Right." he clears his throat, "So, the hospital called."

My stomach fills with dread, feeling like knots tying themselves tighter and tighter. I know what that means.

"They need to do more tests," he continues, "They want to figure out what has caused this latest series of dizzy spells that you've been having, try to get you out of this wheelchair more often."

Bullshit. I know that he had called up the hospital, demanding they treat me. That's just what he did. The 'fainting' spell he was talking about happened once after a particularly long medicine 'treatment' at home, where I fainted after being disconnected. Now it means that I cannot walk, because I'm likely to have another relapse.

I seemed to be able to stand and walk around just fine a few minutes ago. Figures.

I think about arguing about it, refusing to go to the hospital with him. I know it would be more needles, more IVs, more of my father crying to anyone who would listen about how “his baby is always sick, why won’t anyone help me”. But I know that anything I said would fall upon deaf ears. It always did.

I dip my head quietly. He always got his way. I just had to quietly work on my plan to get out, to tell the truth. To someone who would listen.

“When?” I ask.

“As soon as possible,” Father replies. “If you’re ready?”

I nod again - now was not the time to try to defy him.

I begin collecting my things together, no doubt that it would be an extended stay with my father involved. He always tried to find something else for them to investigate, some other scan to potentially find something wrong. I take the photographs from the frame down - it was nice to bring them with me. A snapshot from a happier time. I tuck the latest photograph into the collection - it was risky to leave it out where it could be found. Maybe I’d also have the opportunity to show it to a doctor or nurse if my father ever left my side. Unlikely.

“What is this?”

I freeze. His voice comes from behind me. Where

the letter was. The one I had begun writing just today. The one that would expose everything.

I turn slowly, and try to keep my face neutral to not reveal any fear or worry. He is holding the crumpled version of the beginning of the letter that I had scrapped, one of the many but one of the only ones that I wasn't able to burn. It had fallen into the waste paper bin underneath my desk, beneath where I had stashed it to be hidden from sight. I try to stay calm.

"I...," I say, and try to keep my voice as calm as I can, "I've started a diary."

He pauses for a moment. Did he believe me?

"Why did you not use a notebook?" he asks quietly, as if testing me to see if my answer made sense.

"I-I couldn't find a clean notebook," I hesitate - it was the best answer I can come up with quickly, but wasn't a good one, "Just needed to get my thoughts in order."

"Why was it in the bin?" he asks.

"I-uh-," I try to think fast, "I messed up on the spelling, I threw it away."

Weak excuse. I know it wouldn't be enough.

His eyes slowly move from me to the letter, and darts back to me as if to check my reaction. I try to keep my face neutral, to not show any sign of what I was about to do. I lunge forward, trying to grab the paper from his hands.

Better to be in trouble for not listening to him than reading what I was planning to do.

Too slow.

In one swift movement, he lifts up the letter so I can't reach, and then slaps me hard across the face, and sends me spinning to the ground. The arm closest to the floor pulsates with pain as it lands awkwardly, and causes me to cry out. A sharp pain from my face makes me wince and I blink back tears; I try not to show how much his attack had affected me. When I feel my face, I feel the scratch, and pull back my hand to see that blood has started to pool around it, where his ring cut me.

We stay like that for a moment - him stood with his hand still raised, letter clasped in the other, me with my bloodied hand on my face looking up at him from the floor - before he lowered his hand and looked at the letter.

"To whom it may concern-" he starts reading aloud, "My name is Melanie Mayer and-"

I close my eyes; I know what was coming next.

"-and I have to tell someone this," he continues,

and speaks the words slowly as he processes them, "My father is -"

He pauses, and reads the next words in silence. I know what they said, and what it will mean for me.

My father is poisoning me.

It is true. But did he know that it is? The delusion is intense, so I don't know what his reaction will be. Will he be angry? Sad? Violent? Will this be news to him and he will accept it, or will he deny it?

He continues to read in silence; the muscles in his body tenses. I try to back up slowly and subtly, but there is only so much I could do. I know I don't want to be anywhere near him.

"Lena."

I froze. The tone in his voice seems calm, but I know how dangerous that could be. Hiding beneath the surface.

"Yes?" I whimper; I try to hide my nervousness.

"Where were you going to send this?" he replies, still in that calm and slow tone, as if every word was thought about carefully before speaking them.

"Nowhere," I stumble over the words, trying to find some way to explain what I had written without angering him, "L-Like I said, it's a diary entry. I don't actually believe that, it was in a moment of anger. Nothing-"

"*Nothing?*" I flinch as he suddenly raises his voice, and pulls me up hard by my wrists. I shout in pain as I feel my shoulder creak from the sudden pressure, "*How. Dare. You.*"

I try to begin to apologise, and try to find the words to explain away the things I had begun to write, but he stops me to shout again.

"*I care for you, I do everything to help you,*" he screams in my face, spittle from his mouth spraying in my eye, "*And this is what you do to thank me?*"

"I'm sorry, I'm sorry!" I weep, trying to get to my feet to relieve some pressure from my arm, "I didn't mean it, I was just frustrated of being ill, I don't-"

He cuts me off, pulls me by my arm and pushes me firmly into the wheelchair next to me. I land with a thud, pain begins to throb lower in my back from the impact. He storms out of the room without another word, leaving me sitting breathing heavily; I try not to let the tears fall too fast down my face.

After a moment, I collect the scattered photographs off the floor, and tuck them into my jacket pocket. Something that I know my father would try to take from me. Something that I cannot cope without.

From downstairs, I hear breaking wood, smashing glasses, tearing fabric. I have never known him to be this angry. It is no longer safe for me to stay here - not that it ever was.

How can I get out? The lift? No, that is too noisy. The window? I look out of the window down and wince - no way I can get down safely from the second floor. The stairs? Risky, as I will likely have to interact with my father, in addition to needing to walk down the stairs. If there is anything my father hates, it was when I walked around instead of using my chair.

No. I have to avoid him, but the stairs seem like the only option.

I grab the small wallet from under my bed, containing the money that I had managed to save up from petty cash I had been given in hospital for drinks. There isn't much, but it should allow me to escape the area and get a bus or taxi out.

I listen for a moment to see if I can figure out where my father is currently. Judging by the shouting, he is most likely on the floor below me, so it will have to be a quick run once I got down the stairs. I brace myself, and I try to muster the energy that I will need for the trip. After all, I'm not exactly known for being a marathon runner.

I step out of my room: trying to avoid creaking floorboards and making noise with my footprints. I pause often, listening and continuing on when I am as confident as I can be. Despite moving slowly, I am able to make my way quickly to the stairs. Now is the difficult part.

The stairs.

I hesitantly take the first step and slowly put all my weight down on it. No creak. I take another step. Nothing. One foot after another, I slowly descend the stairs, taking my time to ensure I don't make too much noise. I hold my breath until I got to the bottom, and let out a quiet sigh of relief, once I reach the bottom.

The shouting is louder now, and I am even able to make out some of what he was saying.

"How dare she..."

"Just trying to help her..."

I know that any minute, he could come and speak to me again upstairs, so I have to get out quickly. The door is right there, the portal to my new life. I quickly but carefully weave my way between the medical boxes, the ones filled with the 'life saving' medicine I needed, stacked high until I reach the door. I eagerly turn the handle, excited that I am finally there, only to find that it will not open.

Locked. Shit.

I know exactly where the key was - my father

always hung it on the same hook in the kitchen entranceway, exactly adjacent to the door where my father's study is. Where he currently is.

I breathe deeply, plotting my route through the boxes and into the kitchen. I will go left, then right, then straight. Take the key from the hook, return and unlock the door. Quietly open the door and run. Easy peasy. At least in theory.

I brace myself and start. Left. Right. Straight. I am in the kitchen. Key on the hook on the right. I take it, stashing it quickly in my pocket so the keyring will not jingle in my hands. Now the way back. Straight. Left. Right?

As I walk the last few steps around the boxes, my feet are unsteady. I am home free, ready to escape. Relief flooded my body, my entire body feeling lighter.

Then, I wobble.

I knock one of the boxes from the stack to the floor. I go to catch it, but my reaction is too slow. It falls to the ground with a loud thud.

I freeze, the relief turning quickly to dread. The shouting in the other room ceases. My breath stops as I listen, waiting to hear the footsteps to come towards me. My stomach turns and the urge to vomit comes again as I hear them.

I turn and run towards the door, taking the keys out of my pocket. I try the lock, hands shaking. I have never used this key before, it was always my father who had locked and unlocked the door. I try to stay calm. It is too late.

I hear my father shout my name as he enters the room, and I hear his tell-tale footsteps from behind me. I feel the pinprick on my neck, and all went black.

I was back in the attic; I remembered everything. Even after that moment at the front door. I faded in and out of consciousness, vaguely remembering when I was taken up to this attic.

My memories were back and flashbacks were hitting me from every direction. I remembered throwing the glass mirror across the room, hearing the loud shatter as it broke into pieces. In anger, I had taken the photographs from my pocket, my hands slipping on the smooth paper, and thrown them around myself.

I remember the pain of my knuckles and the cuts, from hitting the trapdoor over and over again in an attempt to persuade my father to come back.

The splinters I got under my fingernails from scratching.

My mother leaving. Trying to get me back. I wonder what my father told her after this - does she think I'm dead? Run away? Stuck in some hospital morgue.

My brother going off to war and never coming home. The pain.

The relief of the trapdoor opening to see my father, only for him to slam the door quickly when he saw I was awake. I didn't eat for a few days after that incident.

The one thing I couldn't remember was how I would escape. Maybe I never knew.

My eyes started to feel heavy. It was still early - the light from the skylight was beaming from above - but I was tired. I ate the last piece of food, deciding to throw the plate across the room where it shattered. It helped me feel a bit better, destroying a piece of what my father had given me.

Unsatisfied, I used one of the pieces of cutlery to scratch out the face where I sat in the wheelchair, not wanting to look again at the haunted look in my eyes. Not that they would help me now.

I piled up the remaining photographs neatly into

a pile and lay back down in my resting place, crying myself into the blissful release of sleep.

Ash. Rotten wood. Stale air. The faint smell of metal.

These were the first things that I noticed when I awoke. My mind tried to connect the dots, tried to link the smells, butI soon realised I had no idea. No memory. Not even my name.

OUT IN THE COLD

STUART WAKEFIELD

Great Plains, Montana, 1887

The boss's room is warm, the crackle of the dying fire peppering his snores.

Today it's cold, colder than ever. It's an unforgiving hand across your face, a slap that makes your cheeks sting like hell. And I'm worried the boss's fire'll be out soon, so I sneak in real quiet, so he can go on sleeping.

He's sprawled naked on his bed, his skin a patchwork of bruises, tattoos of pain, and the cold's nipped it red and raw in places. God made his body, but hard work sculpted it into something that seems unbreakable.

This winter's hard and brutal, burning your

hands and feet, baring its teeth to swallow you whole, but the boss ain't about to be stopped by no blizzard, so he works his spread, day in, day out. I never knew another man who works as hard as the boss.

The first time I saw him sprawled out like this, looking like he had pain tattooed all over his body, I panicked, wanted to call for help, but he told me to hush and get a bowl of warm water and the liniment he used to heal himself up. He was right, of course. Once he was clean and the liniment put on, and the bandages applied, he healed right up. He went out the next day, too, back out into the spread to run his cattle. He makes a good living from the ranch, and he likes being out here in the Judith Basin with the Bear Paw Mountains looking over us from the north like they're holding their breath, waiting for something.

In the spring and summer, the Basin spreads wide and lush below the mountains, covered in swaying prairie grass like an emerald sea, flat and wide, and home to the biggest cattle spreads in the state.

I go to his fire, then open it up real slow so I won't wake him. He needs to rest. From time to time, even though it's not my place, I tell him he should rest, but he goes right on working. Even in a winter like this, one that keeps coming and coming. I take the driest log from the ones I'd stacked that morning, then place it on fading embers, topped with a layer of white as crisp as the snow outside. He's got a book clasped in his left hand—my Bible, its pages worn down from me reading it night after night. If he rolls onto it, it'll wake him, so I take it from his hand real slow, then put it on his nightstand, careful not to knock the lamp, and put out the flame. He rolls onto his left side, letting go of my Bible and curling an arm in under his neck and making a sound in his throat just like an old dog does after it gets comfy in its bed. There are fresh bruises on his ribs and his hips. My eyes linger on the place between his legs, and I get that feeling I don't want to talk about with anyone but God—the thoughts I have at night when I'm alone in my bed in the dark and can't sleep for thinking about him. I tug a sheet over him, more for me than him, then I see it—a deep cut in his shoulder. It ain't bleeding, but it could open up at any time. *Should I wake him?*

I look from him to the window, then decide to let him sleep. I can always stitch it when he wakes up, so I get to closing the curtains against the white nothing outside.

There's an animal call I don't like the sound of. I stop moving and listen. Whatever it is, it might like the light or movement or the smell of the food I'm cooking. If I move real slow, I might get that last curtain closed, and the lamp dimmed so the critter'll be on its way. I confess my hand shakes when I stand behind that last curtain and push real careful. The cry comes again, but further away this time. I still move slow. A movement in the corner of its eye might turn it around and bring it right back, and I don't have time to be fighting off no wolf when I have chores to do.

I could fight. He'd taught me that. How to defend myself if someone attacks. How to defend myself if something comes out of the dark and wants a piece of me. But it wasn't just about defense. He taught me to hunt and shoot. He did most of the hunting part because he soon caught on to the fact it didn't sit right with me. I didn't like killing God's creatures but we had to eat, and I knew it. He said that God wouldn't have put 'em on Earth 'less he'd wanted us to eat 'em. I kept my feelings to myself and I told him he was right, but the look he gave me told me I hadn't won him over.

Didn't matter much. My job is to take care of

him and do as I'm told, and I do both 'em things with all the skill I have—tells me I'm a natural.

I came to work for him at seventeen, traveling east from Highwood with a ranch hand called Laurie. Laurie had done something bad—I didn't ask what—and I hitched a ride with him out of town.

"You don't look like much," the boss had said after he hired Laurie then got a look at me. "What're you good for?"

"I can cook." I'd learned that from watching Momma. "And I ran the house when she got sick."

"Boys don't run houses—that's a woman's job—but there ain't too many women left in these parts."

So he took me on, and I cooked for him and his ranch hands, kept the place clean—his and the bunkhouse—did the laundry, pumped water, chopped wood. It might not have been working the spread, but it was hard work.

One year later, and he's still as stiff in the spine when he speaks as he was that first day. All bottled tension and rigid jaw. All rush to get outside, work his spread, and rear his cattle. And after, when he's slumped by the fire, head dropped, blunted from exhaustion, I wonder how a man so rough can look so soft.

Billy, one of the ranch hands, told me that first summer that the boss once had a wife, but she hadn't cooked or cleaned as well as me.

"Got herself killed," Billy said, tying up his horse, "by a wolf when she was mendin' the barn door instead of makin' his supper. *That* was her job. She didn't have no business fixin' nothin'."

In a picture on the mantle, the woman's face is a perfect oval in black and white. She looks tiny, but so beautifully formed, fair hair, fair skin, but with hard eyes. And I can't bring my eyes to meet hers. They bear down on me, even though she's looking out at a different time. She's there and she's not there, a ghost that's not quite figured out what it is. And her photograph tells me things, reminds me of how little I move in the world. How little I understand it. How little I understand myself.

And so he and I go on. I work inside and he works outside, and that's the way things are.

The critter outside makes another sound, a howl, from farther away. Coyote? Wolf? I guess we're safe for now. Let it take someone else's food.

"You all right?"

I jump at him speaking, and the curtain pole rattles for a moment.

"What's got you so jumpy?" he says, pulling

himself up to sitting, planting his hands on either side of him, then sliding back so he leans against the wall. His voice is gruff, like he's speaking from the back of his throat.

"I heard something, is all, but it's gone now."

He frowns, serious like. "Sumthin'?"

"Something cried out. A coyote or wolf or something, but it's moving away. I closed the curtains so we didn't attract it. Was gonna dim your lamp to make sure."

He pulls the sheet away. "It's hotter than hell in here. You been stokin' the fire?"

"Yes, Boss. I thought there was a chill. Sorry if I—"

He waves his hand for me to stop talking. "Reckon ya mean well, but what I'm feelin' an' what you're feelin' is two different things." His hand reaches up to the right side of his face, fingertips on the skin like he's feeling for a fever.

I take a step forward. "You got a real bad cut in your shoulder. What happened?"

He waves me away. "Ain't nothin' for ya to worry about. What I'm wantin' is sumthin' to eat."

"But it looks deep, needs stitching."

"Quit fussin'."

"Yes, Boss. I got a stew cooking. Thought it'd be

best on a night as cold as this. Been in for a couple of hours, so meat should be soft just like you like it."

"*Soft*? You make me sound like a baby. Tender is better than *soft*. Don't be sayin' *soft* in front of the boys when they're back in spring. They'd be jumpin' over anythin' that gave 'em reason to kick yer ass."

"Yes, Boss."

The deep creases across his brow and around his lips fold, pulling his mouth into a grimace. "And don't be lookin' so sad. You ain't done nothin' wrong. I'm just tellin' ya to watch what ya say in front of people. Ya talk free with me, ya hear?"

"Yes, Boss. Would you like to eat in here? I can bring in a tray."

He swings his legs, solid as iron pipes, over the side of the bed, leaving them open. I look away.

His feet hit the bare boards with a thud and he huffs. "What's got ya so shy? Just a man's body. Ain't nothin' unnatural about that."

"Yes, Boss."

"You got me some fresh clothes?"

I go to his dresser and take out the wool pants he likes to wear in the evenings, faded and creased from a thousand days' wear, then gather up the soft leather shoes I made for him last month.

"You need help dressing?"

“Quit yer fussin. We got whiskey?”

“Getting low.”

“So we have whiskey?”

“Yes, Boss.”

“Pour me some and pour yerself some. Ya did good work today. Place never looked so clean. Was lucky to find someone who works as hard as ya. Could go on usin’ ya for a few years more.”

“That’s a fine compliment, Boss. I’ll get dinner on the table and pour you—us—that whiskey.”

I make my way out of his room and go to the kitchen.

I was lucky to find someone like you.

Those weren’t the words he used, but that’s what I take from ’em.

I can’t say I want to be *used*. Tools get used. I want something more than that. I want kissing and touching and the like. Something soft and loving. I ain’t had love in—well—ever. Not that life at home wasn’t one of being cared for, but love? Love wasn’t a part of my life. Not for me and not for my brothers and sisters. No one ever talked about it as far as I can remember, but I reckon it was something we all wanted. Just that no one said it. We got sent to school and got three meals a day. Those were our days. We prayed a little every evening, but Sundays were for morning prayer that went on a little longer. Everyone in town gathered and prayed to be good people. Praying went right up to the day I left to work at the ranch and I went right on with it. It gave me comfort knowing God was looking out for me. Even here. Even through the hardest days and nights. Days working and nights dreaming. I knew my kind of dreaming wasn't what God wanted for me, but He kept me from touching myself and I told myself that was enough.

We don't talk over dinner. The stew's good, a feast of beef, heart and liver, but I left out the brains and guts, adding beans instead. I ain't never liked brains nor guts. He bows his head when he gets to eating and he eats like a man who's been out in the cold all day. Sometimes I half expect his head to split apart and take his food down in one gulp. When it comes to speaking, after dinner is another matter.

"Even colder out there," he says with a shiver, looking toward the window. "A lot o' cattle drifted into Limestone Canyon. Didn't have the sense to dig down, find the grass. Starved to death. Froze right where they were standin'." He looks down at his rough hands, still a little brown from the hot, dry summer that brought drought and prairie fires. "Got some strays to a spot where the wind had blown the snow clear, but most of 'em is dead."

He'd hoped the winter'd be mild, but the geese flew south and the cottonwood trees grew thicker bark. The snow came in November and apart from a warm spell in December, it just kept a'coming.

"How was yer day?" he says, like he wants to stop thinking on things.

"Don't have much to say that you ain't heard before."

He grunts just the once. "What about when ya was a kid? What was that like?"

I tell him about Momma and my siblings and the church. That I *can* talk about. What I don't tell him about is the kiss between me and Owen Wiley, the reason I left town. "It's not exciting, I know."

But he seems to like learning about my life. Nodding and the like. I guess we're living together in our own way, so it's natural he'd want to know more. He seems to like me enough. I mean, he's letting me take whiskey with him—that has to count for something.

"Read some of ya storybook," he says, "before I got to sleepin'."

"It was right there in your hand until it put it on

your nightstand. You thinking of becoming a God-fearing man?"

He huffs. "God don't want no man like me."

He always calls my Bible my *storybook*. I don't mind. If he doesn't have faith, he doesn't have faith, and that's all there is to it. It's not my place to put him right. It's not my place to do anything but take care of him. A part of me wants that care to be spiritual, but I never dare speak of it to him like that. If he reads the Bible and takes pleasure or comfort, then so be it.

"Story about Daniel and them lions," he says. "Reminds me of here, I guess. Got myself into spots I'd rather not have been in. Before yer time, though, and I learned not to get in 'em again." He glances at the window again. "Seems like every year it gets colder. Like nature wants its land back"

"Makes sense, I guess. We went against—"

"God's plan?"

I fall quiet.

"Reckon ya got yer faith, but there ain't no God in town and there sure as shit ain't no God out here. If there was, he wouldn't have left us to rot."

"You came out here. Why was that?"

His back goes rigid, and I know I've spoken out of turn.

"Reckon I jest don't like folks. An' sure as hell don't need their sympathy." His eyes flicker to his wife's picture, then he looks down at his whiskey and sighs. His voice is rough, like sandpaper. His words aren't full of venom, just honest. "Sorry for what I said about yer god. Guess I'm jealous because I can't find no comfort in it."

My heart sinks. "You can't?"

"Not one bit. I'd like it though. Life's hard enough without wantin' a little pleasure in life."

Pleasure's so close I can feel it, smell it. He's got his own magnetic field, and any time he draws near my heart gets to beating fast.

"You don't like it here?" I say.

"Like it fine." He looks at me for a minute. "Sometimes it doesn't feel enough, is all. You ever feel like that?"

Most nights.

"I take pleasure in what I do and doing it well. Like when you said you liked the place when you woke and gave me this here whiskey and being able to drink it with you. I take pleasure and comfort in that, I guess."

"Ya *guess*? Don't ya know?"

I don't like where this is headed. "Maybe not. I make comfort, but I don't know if I feel it."

"Reckon that's real sad. For both of us."

The clock chimes nine.

He drains the last of his whiskey, then puts down his glass. "Best be turnin' in. Early start."

He says it like it's something new. Every day is an early start.

Picking up the bottle, I wish him goodnight. He stands, stretches, his pants snug against his skin, his hard slab of stomach barely showing a curve through the fabric. He gives me a nod as if he's passing me on the street, then goes to his room.

In the kitchen, I pour my whiskey back into the bottle. It smells fine and warm, like a wooden barrel on a summer day, and I can't stomach seeing it go to waste. I wash the glasses, then set 'em aside to drain.

I can't find the comfort in it. You ever feel like that?

The thoughts I shouldn't be having come back to me as though I hadn't thought 'em in years. Why does he say things like that to me? I'm here to take care of him, not to give him the answers to questions like that. How can you ask someone to comment on their feelings when they're not supposed to have any?

I'm not, am I? Not when it comes to him. I have a job to do and that's all there is to it.

I lay in bed, awake and staring into the darkness. I should be reading my Bible, but it's on his nightstand in his warm room next to his warm body in his warm bed. I close my eyes and get to praying, finding it hard to concentrate without my mind wandering back to what he said.

That's real bad. For both of us.

That's the first time he's referred to him and me as *us*. There is no *us*. There's him and his work and me and my work. We're not a team. I serve him and he serves himself. That's the order of things.

In the morning, he's up and gone even though there's barely light outside. I check the pantry to make sure he's taken the food I packed him—beef jerky and sourdough biscuits. I clean his room, haunted by the smell of him, touching his sheets, his pillow, his clothes, everything I can grasp or hold.

Yesterday's clothes—washed clean of mud and blood—have gone from his chair.

I strip his sheets and pillowcases, fold 'em into a rough pile, then put on new. I carry the old ones into the kitchen, then get to the cleaning. I dry dust, then sweep and mop before getting to wiping down the counters and emptying his bedpan. Weather's too bad to use the outhouse.

Outside, the only sounds are my boots sinking into the snow and the creak of the porch. The cold's a claw, each breath pawing at my lungs, and it's cut out the sound of everything around it.

I clear the porch of snow, keeping an eye out for him, but it snowed again this morning, and his tracks have gone. Even the shape of the wagon he moved out of the barn to make room for the horses is gone, choked by white. He's supposed to tell me what direction he's going in, so if something happens I can go looking, but never does. He don't have no routine neither so I can't get to guessing where he is. He's funny like that. Don't want no one keeping tabs on him. Not even me.

In the springhouse I chop wood, every muscle in my arms shivering, but I keep at it until I've split enough to get us through the next week. I carry it inside, shaking the snow off my boots and cursing myself for having to mop the floor again.

And his wife's staring down at me from the mantle. Looking at me with her icy, hard eyes like she hates me for what I really am, what I've always been. Like she's spit her hatred into her mouth but had to swallow it on account of not being able to speak.

I tell myself I can fight it. That I'm stronger than

my feelings for him, but sometimes I feel myself slipping. And I have to fight the urge to do something that I know I'll regret.

Putting the photograph facedown, I carry on with my chores.

Dinner's beef from the icehouse—seems like everywhere's the icehouse these days—and potatoes from the root cellar. It's what he likes, and I'm in no position to argue otherwise. He kicks up a fuss if I make something else for long. He's stubborn like that. Tell him to turn left, and he'd be sure to turn right just to prove he's his own man. I cooked the meat real slow, so it's soft—sorry, *tender*—like he likes it. I have to smile at that. Like soft meat made *him* soft. He's the toughest man I ever met, which made it all the more strange he'd talked about comfort last night. Pleasure, yes, but comfort? He'd blindsided me with that. At least I know the struggle's not my own to bear and he's dealing with the same.

The day's gone before I know it, and he's back an hour after sundown. He washes in his room, but he doesn't call for me to do his back. He doesn't speak during dinner or after and he goes to bed without a word. I get the nod that he likes his food—he's got some manners—but that's it.

I clean up like I always do, then I wash his bedding, leaving his clothes until last, so the mud and blood doesn't stain the sheets. I hang everything out to dry in front of the fire for mending and folding in the morning.

When I go to my room, my Bible's on my pillow. The leather cover's cold. I hold it to my face, hoping to smell his hands on it or his breath on its pages. I should be glad to have it back, but now it's like having God in my room, his eyes on me, scolding me for all my failures and loneliness. It's a long time before I get to sleeping.

When it comes to cleaning and cooking, the next day's the same, except I have the mending to do. However he hurt himself the day before, it made a real mess of his clothes. His shirt, undershirt, and pants all need darning. I sit by the window where it's brightest and get to work. There's a certain kind of peace to it. The thought it takes nudges everything else aside. I'm lost in it for a couple of hours, so dinner'll be something fast. Steak, I'm thinking, and I'll use the fat to make a sauce too. That'll get him talking.

I'm right.

"Mighty fine," he says after his first mouthful,

and he's right—just the right amount of char on the outside and pink in the middle.

The conversation stops there. Is he mad at me for something? I can't think of a chore I missed. I scrubbed the floors, mended his clothes ... Everything. I did everything and more.

"Thank you, Boss. I made a pie if you'd like some."

He stops eating. "A pie?"

"Apple, kinda, 'cept I used crackers. We didn't have no apples."

"Crackers?" He says, screwing up his face. "A cracker pie."

"I swear you'll never know it ain't real apples."

"An apple pie. How goddamn American can ya get?" He finishes the last of his steak, wipes his mouth, then puts down his napkin. "Will it keep?"

"For what?"

"That ain't my question. Will it keep?"

"Yes, but—"

"For how long?"

"A week I guess."

He throws his fork onto his plate, wipes a sudden sweat from his brow, then covers the fork with his napkin. "Riders comin'. Saw 'em today. Far off, but I saw 'em all the same. Means they're comin'. Always means they're comin'. And when they do, we fight 'em, drive 'em off, and celebrate with that pie."

He told me about 'em once. How they ambushed him when he was out in the field tending some kind of crop—it weren't important to the story, even though I asked.

"Took me by surprise," he'd said, stoking the dying fire himself, staring at it as though he was trying to bring it back to life. "Which is strange for riders, seein' as no one taught 'em how to creep up on a man."

"Were you frightened?"

He laughed but there weren't no joy in it. "Didn't have time for fright. Had two tryin' to hold me still and a gun pointed square at my chest. That was their first mistake. Should'a had it pointed in my face. Still, stamped on one's foot, then pulled him in front of me when he bent down in pain. Rider with the gun shoots in fright. Takes the head clean off his friend. One with the gun got to retchin'. I dipped under the other's arm, got myself behind him, and used him as a batterin' ram to knock the gunman down. A stamp on one's neck and a bullet in the other, and it was over. Lookin' back, it was kinda fast, but it didn't feel like it at the time. Time felt real slow, like the sun's on yer bed in the mornin' and all ya want to do it stretch and roll over and sleep some more. You know that feelin'?"

I couldn't say I did. Well, not alone, anyways, but I'd thought about waking up with him an awful lot, our bodies side by side or one curled into the other.

"What did you do with the bodies?" I asked.

"Dragged 'em outside for the wolves."

But the riders don't come and life goes on as normal, but I double down on my chores just to keep my mind off the thought of strangers bringing trouble to our door. And all the time I'm cleaning, I know his dead wife's watching me like I'm her and she's the wolf. I bow my head, not wanting to see her. When he's gone and it's just me and her, I swear I can hear her breathing. She hates me for loving him like she was born to it.

"Sweet Jesus," he says when he comes in that night. "Thought ya worked hard, but this? This looks like a palace. Everything's so—shiny. How'd ya do that?"

I don't think he's waiting on an answer—it's not like he's ever gonna to pick up a cloth and do it himself—but I flush with pride, the feeling spilling out and making my skin as warm as the sun.

Sure enough, he goes on. "Weather got real bad this past hour. Might have to dig ourselves out tomorrow. Ya good at digging?"

"Guess it can't be harder than chopping wood when you can't even feel your hands." He laughs, then winces a little. "I forget how green ya still are, this bein' yer first bad winter an'all. And I ain't talkin' about a few extra inches, I'm talkin' about *feet,* ya got a wall of it lookin' back at ya. Either way, you're gonna be moppin' like ya never mopped before." I try to imagine snow that deep, but I'm tired from chores so my mind's not up to the task. "So what do we do?"

Even though I don't want to admit it, digging our way out of the snow seems like a bad idea. It had to be dangerous, but I guess we wouldn't have no choice.

He seems to sense what I'm thinking.

"I'm built for diggin'," he says, "so I don't need no help on that account. It's kinda fun when ya think about it—diggin' yerself out of yer own home."

"Fun? Don't seem like fun to me. Seems like a lot

of things could go wrong doing something like that."

He slaps a hand down on my shoulder. I can feel it through my shirt, heat coming out of him and into me.

He ain't never touched me before. Now, his hand's clamped down on me like the jaws of a critter who's fancying to take a chunk out of me, then a few chunks more. A part of me likes it, but the part of that don't wins out. I take a step back, twisting out from under that hand and making for the stove.

"Wipe that frown off yer face," he says, low and breathy. "Ain't as dangerous as it sounds. Ya worry too much. Might not even come to that if things ease up. What's for dinner?"

"Ribs. Just how you like 'em."

"Ya make everythin' how I like it. I got time to clean up first?"

"Yes, Boss."

"Nothin's ever too much trouble, is it? Just how I like it—nice and simple."

"The way I see it, you got enough outside that ain't nice or simple. Least I can do is keep things running smooth in here."

"That ya do. Say, ya mind helpin' me with my dressin' after? Smells kinda funny."

He sets out towards his room, shucking off his jacket, great chunks of snow falling off his boots and dirtying up my clean floor. I set out the ribs to let ’em rest, then go clean up the mess. His clothes are dumped in a ragged line down the hallway, each one thrown off him like they’re chains he’s escaping from, and I bundle ’em all up, squeezing the last of their warmth against me.

He’s grumbling about something. Water’s splashing and spilling each time he makes angry sounds from deep in his chest. Never heard a man growl like him. Not ever.

Then there’s a thump, then it all goes quiet. No water, no growling, no nothing. I drop his clothes, then lean into the door. “You okay in there?”

“Reckon,” he says, his words slowing, “things are kinda bad.”

It gives a little, then stops. I’m worried to shove it. He’s on the floor, I reckon. If I push the door too hard, I might catch a part of him and hurt him some more. I lean in again, going real easy, and get the door open just enough so as I can squeeze through the gap. He’s lying on his front, head turned towards me, eyes shut. He’s out cold, but he’s still breathing. The dressing on his back’s shifted some. The skin underneath’s a mess. Blackened and ragged at the edges—he told me it didn't need no stitching—and there's a yellow fluid running from it.

I know this ain't right and I'm scared. I'm not sure if it's the fluid or if it's the sight of him lying there unconscious like that, but no matter what it is, it's got me cornered.

I do my best to get him upright and leaning sideways against the bed without hurting him, but I graze his good shoulder a little. Not so much that I draw blood, but I reckon it's bad enough for him to be asking questions when he comes around.

Getting the dressing off's easy enough, seeing as the muck's worked its way through the sticky stuff, shifting the dressing enough for infection to get in. I take the washbasin, then tip it out the window, the cold reaching its claws into the room before I shut 'em out. Once I fill it with clean water from the jug, I grab a clean cloth.

He's right where I left him, which is some relief seeing as the wound's open to the air. I might be good at cleaning, but a floor's a floor and carries things even elbow grease can't shift. I bathe the wound. It's edges are charred, and it's wet, shifting with fluids. I get the liniment from the pantry's top shelf, and I'm about to change the dressing when I remember the whiskey. Reckoning it can't make matters no worse, I fetch it from the pantry then take it back to him. I get a grunt and a moan when I pour a little of the whiskey in the wound, but he's in no position to be cussing at me for causing him pain. When the wound's looking as dry as it's gonna get, I apply the fresh dressing. It takes me a little under five minutes to get him from his room to the parlour. I fetch my mattress, put it in front of the fire, then thicken it up with cushions and blankets until it's as thick as his bed. There's no elegance to it, but I haul him onto the makeshift bed, then pour him a fresh glass of water. In the firelight, his skin's yellow, like a newspaper that's been left in the sun. I hold his head against my chest so I can ease his jaw open a little, then tip the water so it wets his tongue. His mouth works to suck the water in, so I know he's got something left in him. It all goes down smooth enough, then I roll him onto his chest with his head turned to the side so he can breathe.

I settle into a chair and wait. If he gets to shivering or sweating or shallow breathing, we've got trouble. If it's that, then I gotta go get help. That's a medical thing and I ain't no doctor.

And I wouldn't think twice about going out in the cold and getting help. I wouldn't even think once. I'd just do it. For him. I'm given to being attached, so attachment's all I got.

His breathing's quiet, like a child playing hide-and-go-seek, then it's muffled and laced with pain, turning ragged.

"Not unless I die," he blurts.

I sit up. "What?"

"I said, not unless I die. Ya ain't getting on no horse in this weather."

He's talking nonsense, so I play along. "So that's what you gotta do. You gotta get better. So I don't have to go out in it."

"Ain't dying on no horse. And ain't dying in front of you neither."

"Hush yourself, now. Just breathe like you're sleeping." It's not long before his breathing slows. I put another blanket on him, then get his jacket and put that on too.

Maybe I should cool him off, not cover him up.

Fetching a clean cloth and cold water, I soak his brow, close enough to count his eyelashes, fighting with everything I've got not to stroke 'em. He mewls like a kitten, so I reckon cooling him off is right and I take off the jacket and blanket.

I get up, get the bottle of whiskey and a glass, then sit by his side, my feet tucked up under me. I take a swig of the whiskey and my throat's as warm as a bug in the sun.

I'm thinking how it's been years since I've sat still. Years since I've had someone to sit still with. Years since I've had someone I needed to stay still for.

I nurse the whiskey and watch him. He's sleeping hard now. *I'm not gonna let you die.*

And at the thought of death, I look up at that damn picture of his wife and the whiskey goes from warm to hot like I'm swallowing drawn blood. I don't want to think about her, in his bed, beneath his sheets, naked for him. I don't want to think about that, so I take another slug.

I'm getting drunk. But there's a funny thing about knowing you're drunk. It makes things real clear. I'm real clear about how I feel about him. I'm feeling much more than I'm meant to be, and I don't know what to do with that.

I take another swig.

He's the thing that matters.

I look at him, and I know.

I know.

I'm not gonna let him die.

My throat's furry with the taste of whiskey.

I press my tongue against the roof of my mouth, feeling its cotton thickness, then the ridges of my teeth. I feel the knot of my stomach and the sting of my temples. My head's pounding.

He cracks open an eye. "Y'all right?"

I can't help but laugh a little. "You're asking me? You're the one flat out on the parlour floor."

He lifts his head. "Don't get it." He rolls over, but I don't get to him in time. "Shit!" he says when his dressing touches the mattress. "What in the—?"

I roll him onto his side. "Remember that cut you wouldn't let me stitch?"

"Yeah?"

"Well, it got infected."

His breath catches in his throat and his face twists like he's fighting to swallow. "Is this the part where ya tell me *I told ya so*?"

"Would it help?"

"Not one bit."

He makes to get up, but I push him back down.

"Then I'm saying nothing. You gotta rest, though. I guess I need to be feeding them horses of yours. You got any cattle nearby?"

His mouth opens, he draws in a breath, and his chest expands. He's not been breathing right all night, so I take it as a good sign. "How long ya been watchin' me for?"

Every day since I got here. "Eighteen hours."

He squints slowly, as if not believing a word I'm saying. With effort, he opens his eyes wide, attempting to remove the wrinkles of doubt that have formed between them. "Just the horses. Ya know what to do?"

"Yes, Boss."

"They're gonna be awful hungry." He rubs a hand across his face, wiping the crust from the corners of his mouth, like he's trying to remember something. "Was washin' up before dinner ..."

"That's when you passed out. I cleaned your wound, then got you in here. Once that wound's stopped leaking, I'm gonna stitch you up. No arguments, you hear?"

Huffing through his nose. "Yes, Boss." A smile, crooked and misaligned but real, comes across his face, inching shadows of doubt from his eyes. His eyes show a hint of a spark, a glimmer of light, like a distant candle in a dark room. "You all right?"

I wonder if he knows how much power he holds over me, how much power his kiss might steal from my body, how much power his touch could draw from my heart. "Can't say you didn't give me a fright," I say.

He pushes himself up onto his elbow. "Ya look tired. Ya really been here all this time?"

"Damn right."

His eyes narrow. "You're not all right. Ya said *damn*. Ain't never said *damn* in all the time ya been here."

"I—"

"Ya'd better be prayin' extra hard tonight. God Almighty's gonna be real pissed with ya." He stops for a minute. "Still, savin' a life'll make up for it."

"I didn't save your life."

"Ya reckon? 'Cause from where I'm lookin'—down here on the damn floor—if ya hadn't 'a been here, I'd be in a whole heap o'trouble."

I rest the back of my hand on his forehead. It's warm, but that could just be the fire. His hair's dark with sweat. I want to run my hand along his jawline and tell him not to worry. Instead, I fetch a glass of water from the kitchen. He gulps it, then closes his eyes.

"Better?" I ask. He nods a little. I place my hand back on his forehead. "If it wasn't me, it would have been someone else."

Eyes soft, he looks up at me from under those thick black eyebrows. “Ain’t no one here but us.”

He looks at the photograph, and the look does something to my insides—a little jolt in my belly that turns heavy. His old life was right there on the mantle, just behind the picture—the pulse of all that had happened and the tangled thread of memory.

“You need something to eat,” I say quickly, getting to my feet, my head spinning a little. I steady myself against the mantle. It’s rough under my palm.

His tongue darts across his lower lip. “Maybe them ribs?”

“I’m thinking grits seeing as you missed breakfast. You think you can eat?”

“Ya ever seen me turn down a meal?”

I turn away, my hand running across the mantle’s grain. “I’ll go feed them horses, then put the grits on to heat.”

I bundle myself up in two of everything—socks, shirts, jackets, and pants. The stable’s fifty yards from the cabin, but I reckon it’s far enough to freeze to death. He was right about the weather. It had been creeping toward a snowstorm all of yesterday, and it was during the night when it finally hit, rolling in through the blackness.

I give him one last glance then slip out, wading into snow as deep as my knees, clotting my pants with white, freezing around my legs. I guess where the porch steps might be, getting it half right before stumbling when my left foot comes down on nothing. I lean right, then tumble over into the white. The snow is quiet, peaceful, like mumbling a prayer, and the only sound's my heart beating in my ears. I know I should get back up, but all the fight's gone out of me. Instead, I just lay there. A tear streaks over the bridge of my nose, freezing before it hits the ground, then I get to sobbing, deep and muffled.

Thank you, God. Thank you.

I've eased him off the mattress, then pushed it up against a wall so he's got a little to sit on and a little to lean on. I place a cushion behind his lower back and another behind his neck so the dressing's not touching the wall.

The first spoonful of his grits makes a soft, cloying sound. The second is louder. The third and fourth are the loudest of all.

"We got more?" he says.

"Well, ain't nothing wrong with your appetite. I'll get 'em."

He hands me the bowl. "You all right?"

These days, he's real interested in how I'm doing. Maybe he's avoiding how he's doing.

"You keep asking," I say, "but you're the one who passed out."

He wipes his mouth with the back of his hand, but slow like he's stiff. Avoiding my gaze, he lowers his voice. "You're a little red in the eyes, is all."

Had he heard me sobbing out there in the snow? If he had, what did it mean to him?

I pin his spoon to his bowl with my thumb so it doesn't fall when I'm carrying it. "It's the cold. I ain't used to it. It's like—"

Then he's staring past me like he's seeing something I can't. "Like it's out to get ya?"

He's right. It's like the cold's a killer that just keeps on coming. But it's only a killer if you let it.

"Make sure ya fill that bowl up good," he says, back from wherever he'd gone. "I'm hungry as all out."

In the kitchen, I splash my face with water, then fill his bowl to the brim with grits. If he doesn't finish what's in the pan, I'll take some too.

He eats slow this time, looking at the floor,

through it, like something's on his mind. "Ya see any signs?"

It takes me a moment to get his meaning. "Of riders? Don't think they'd risk this weather. It's gonna be coming down again real soon."

"Good," he says with a quick, fleeting grunt. "Don't want 'em any time soon. Don't want 'em at all."

A soft thud as his bowl hits the floor, and I dart forward to steady it, catching the spoon as it topples over the edge and onto the floor. His head lolls forwards, his breathing slow and shallow like he's giving up, but his chest still moves.

"I need to change that dressing," I say.

"Do what ya gotta to get me back outside," he says, eyes closed. "Got me things to do."

He's leaning forward, elbows on his knees, his eyes screwed up. His wound's still weeping, but I fancy it's less than before. Wishful thinking on my part, I guess.

I do the same as I did the night before. Warm water, whiskey, and a fresh dressing. He cusses at the whiskey—"Wanna drink it, not bath in it."—but he takes the rest well enough.

I wring out the cloth.

"You need to clean up. Dirty skin's not gonna

help with that cut. If I fill up the tub, you wanna bath?"

He nods, so I hook my arms under his and get to lifting him to his feet. He stumbles, nearly taking me with him, but I grab the mantle to keep us from crashing to the floor and my hand brushes the picture. I pull my hand back in a rush like she's not done with me yet, like she's trying to tear my secrets from me and tell him what I really am.

"Weak," he says, breathing hard, warm, and damp on my neck.

"And to think you were gonna dig your way outta here." The air smells of whiskey and stale ash. The whole place needs a bath. "I reckon we got two options. I drag the tub in here or I wipe you down myself."

"Tub," he says, real fast.

"All right, then. Stay here and I'll do what needs doing."

A minute later, I'm in the springhouse, pumping sputtering, crackling water until my shoulders burn. It's hard work at the best of times. In the winter, it's harder still. I fill one bucket, two, three, carrying each one inside, my legs aching like they might fall right off, and it's less than thirty paces to the house.

Then I'm wrestling to get the tub from the

bunkhouse through the back door. It's not the weight, it's the shape—too wide and too deep.

"Ya havin' trouble?" he calls from the parlour, a hint of the desperate in his voice.

What's he fretting about? It's just a bath.

I give up. I'm bright—they told me so at school —but there's no way I can figure out how to squeeze that tub through that door. I go back to the parlour.

His face is set, all grim. "Can't ya shift it?"

"I'll have to wipe you down." And suddenly it hits me that I'm going to be touching him—all of him—even if it's only with a washcloth. Even if it's only parts of his body and not what's inside his heart, I'll still be touching him. My heart's banging against my breastbone like a jailbreak and sweat sluices down my back.

His look darkens as though a turkey buzzard's passing between him and the sun. "Guess there's no choice."

Another bowl of warm water and another washcloth, then I fetch the soap from his washstand.

I kneel beside him, and he leans forward. His skin's dusty with grit. What was I thinking? I should have cleaned him up when he was passed out, but that wouldn't have been proper. I wet the cloth, rub a little soap on it, then start with the back of his neck.

"You need a haircut," I say, trying to distract myself from kissing the stretch of skin. "And a shave."

"Haircut's last of my worries, and my beard only needs trimmin'. I like a beard in the winter."

As I wash his shoulders, I keep my eyes on the parlour floor. If I look at him, I know I'll want to look at more of him. "A trim then. I'll do it when you're feeling better."

"Ain't fixin' on bein' ill for long, so ya'll get your chance soon enough."

I wet the cloth again, then leave his shoulders, running the cloth down his spine, real careful not to drip water down his back. He leans into me and sighs. His skin's dusty, but he's not filthy. He's clinging to the edge of the mattress like he's holding on for his life. His pants are sticking out behind him and I work my way down his back to the dimples at the bottom of his spine. Heat surges through my body, racing away from the pit of my stomach and heading for my ears, and I'm shaking all over. I ain't never touched him like this. I stop just above his waist. I can't touch him there, front or back—I can't touch him in places he doesn't want me to touch.

"How're you feeling?" I say.

"Honest? Like I been rode hard and put up wet."

I wring out the cloth then wipe down his arms. Nothing there except for a couple of yellowing bruises, and he don't make a sound when I move over 'em. "Arm up."

He raises his arm, then sniffs. "Guess it wasn't just that wound that stank."

I rub some extra soap onto the cloth, then spend my time cleaning his armpit.

"Nothing wrong with the smell of a working man," I say.

"How about a workin' man reekin' of infection?"

"Arm down." I move to his other side, my back to the fire. "Now this one." His left arm's dirty but clear of bruises.

"I could be doin' this with my free hand." He's grumpy, but he's still talking. That's something.

"No, you couldn't. Now hold still."

"I'm hardly movin'."

I drag the cloth down his arm. He's quiet for a long time. "You're a strange one."

My hand freezes. "How's that?"

"You're ... You're proper. Ya do what needs doin' and ya don't fuss, and yer as tough as Billy and the rest of 'em. Ya got a purpose, and ya ain't scared of me."

I move some more water around the bowl, then wipe down his left hand, turning my head away. The back of my neck's got the sweat going. I'm not scared of him. I'm scared at the thought of being *with* him.

"Yeah, I reckon so. You're probably right," I say. It's best to agree with him. I don't want him thinking I'm strange. "All right. Gonna wipe your face so close them eyes and look up a little."

The left corner of his mouth twitches. "How can I look up with my eyes closed?"

I wring out the cloth, but only rub the tiniest amount of soap on it in case it gets in his eyes. "You talking back to me?"

"Just tryin' to lift the mood."

Giving him a small smile, I hooked a finger under his chin, wishing it was to bring his lips to mine. "All I need is for you to be lifting your face."

"Yes, Boss." He coughs. "Felt kinda strange sayin' that, but I guess yer in charge right now."

I dab at his sweat-drenched brow, then along his cheekbones. "I don't get how you're this dirty," I say, "when all that's out there is frozen water."

"Plenty of places for me to get dirty."

His lips are firm, with a slight upward curl at the corners, but I reckon he ain't never learned how to smile. I breathe in through my nose, then out through my mouth, dragging the wet cloth over the bridge of his nose. My body shivers. "I don't care to think of the places you get dirty." I drag the cloth down over his stubbled cheeks, and he flinches.

"Sorry," I say. There's a spot on his cheek I can't shift. "What is this?" I say.

He touches it. "Splinter, I guess."

I lean in, trying to work out which angle to ease it out so it don't scratch up his face. "You been fixing that barn door?"

He shakes his head. "Gonna need help. Come out with me when the weather's better."

The warmth of his skin's heating my face as much as the fire's heating my back. We ain't never been this close. Close enough to kiss if we were both accepting of it, but he's for women and I'm for God, so it ain't never gonna happen.

He swallows, and I'm close enough to see the pulse in his neck. I haven't cleaned him there yet, and I get to wondering what the salt from his skin might taste like. Goosebumps raise on my skin, my neck, my arms. My heartbeat, his heartbeat, our breaths, and the fire crackling.

He takes my hand real gentle. "Maybe ya could —" He takes a deep breath, and his eyes dart from my face to my mouth and then back again. "—help me."

I sit back. "Like you said, when the weather's better." Wringing out the cloth, my hands get to shaking. "Head up and I'll do your front."

His brows pinch together, the wrinkles on his forehead etched like a map, then clears his throat, but the sound cracks.

Is he scared of something?

He bundles his hands in his lap. "I can do it."

"This ain't no time for being stubborn. Being stubborn got you into this mess, what with you railing against those stitches."

Raising his head, he closes his eyes. "If I'd had a momma, I'd say ya sounded like her."

This is the first thing he's hinted of his past, and it brings me up short. "What happened to your momma?"

His shoulders come up and then settle back down, his chest rising and falling like a wave on the ocean. "Damned if I know. Same with my daddy. Didn't know either of 'em. My aunt raised me."

I wipe his neck. It's thick and strong and his throat's bobbin' while he talks. I get to thinking I want to kiss him right there. *He's for women and I'm for God.* I wring out the cloth. "Did she treat you good?"

"Only beat me twice a week," he says, laughing himself into a cough.

I get to thinking about what it'd be like to grow up like that. He's a man of the Plains, so he knows how to survive, but regular a beating ain't no way for a boy to grow up.

He looks around the room, then says, "Gotta admit, this ain't how I pictured things comin' together."

"How did you picture 'em?"

He looks up at the ceiling, then down again. "Imagined takin' a wife and havin' a family, not rearin' cattle."

I dab at his chest, wishing a wife hadn't figured at all.

Holding my wrist, he brings me in closer to his face. "I ain't never thanked ya for savin' my life."

Glancing at his shoulder, I clear my thickening throat. "You're welcome."

"Ya could've left me."

"God touched my life. Least I can do is some good with it."

His lips tighten, and he lets go of my wrist.

Stretching my fingers out, I start on the right-hand side of his ribs. “How long were you married?”

“A year,” he says like he doesn’t want to talk about it, but I press on.

“Billy told me what happened to her. I’m sorry.”

He looks at his wife’s photograph for a long time, then holds out his hand. “Help me up. Don’t wanna be sittin’ here no more. Want my bed.”

“But you—”

“This ain’t a negotiation. Help me up.”

I shouldn’t have asked about his wife and got him all riled up.

It takes me a good while to get him to his bed ‘cause he’s weak and weak makes him heavy when he’s slumped against me. I have to hold him up the whole entire time. I lower him real careful until he’s sitting on the edge, then I fetch his bedding.

“Get me some water,” he calls, “and warm up them ribs, and when does this dressin’ need a’changin’?”

I hover in the doorway, one foot out of his room and one foot in; one foot in my feelings and one foot out. “Twice a day’s best.”

“All right, then. I don’t want ya comin’ in here unless it’s to change it, ya hear?”

"Yes, Boss." I don't move, still kicking myself for upsetting him.

"Well," he says, voice sharp. "What is it?"

"I gotta make your bed. And—uh—have I said something or done something out of turn because as God is my witness, I'd never—"

He sighs long and deep. "*God, God, God.* Do the bed, then leave me be."

"Yes, Boss." I make up the bed, then step out of his bedroom, closing the door real slow.

I heat up his ribs, making a thick, black gravy so they don't dry out. Once they're done, I load up a tray with 'em, a jug of water, and a glass.

In his bedroom, I pull up a chair, then set down the tray. He's still lying on his side, but he looks past me and out the window. Neither of us speaks.

I get to my chores, squeezing a day's work into the last few hours of daylight, then feed the horses, making sure their blankets are still tight across their backs.

Back inside, I put meat and potatoes to roasting, then I check the time. It's late—almost nine—so I need to change his dressing.

I dally at his bedroom door, then give it a knock.

"Come on in."

He's picked the ribs clean. Keeping quiet, I set

down the dressings on his nightstand, then take away the tray, leaving the jug and the glass.

He's sitting up when I get back, sipping water. I settle on his right side, then he turns a little so I can get to the old dressing. I peel it back real careful.

"Well?" he says.

"It ain't weeping no more, but it ain't closing up neither."

"Guess I need them stitches after all."

"You sure?"

"Wouldn't be sayin' it otherwise. Go get what ya need."

I go to the kitchen, then boil up some water. I get a needle and thread, pour a little of the boiled water into a shallow dish so it cools off, then take it all back to him.

He takes one look at the alcohol, then shakes his head. "Don't need it."

"It'll hurt."

"Save it for some other time."

Why he wants to suffer is up to him, but if it was me, I'd want the lot poured on me and a wooden spoon in my mouth. "If that's what you want."

I go careful, cleaning out the wound with the water, then stitch, keeping a quarter of an inch between 'em and from the edges of his skin. He's sweating hard but he don't say nothing. I'm careful to pull the stitches tight as I can without puckering the skin. I tie the thread off, rub a little alcohol along the stitches, then cover them with a clean dressing.

"That's it," I say, placing what I've used on the chair ready for taking out.

He lays himself back down, and I make to leave, gathering up the things.

"Take a seat," he says, voice flat. "Got sumthin' to say."

I clear the seat, setting everything on the floor.

He's still looking past me. "Seems I owe you an apology."

"Boss, I—"

"Hush up."

"Yes, Boss."

Shifting where he's lying, he glances at my chest, then looks away. "Been out here a long time. I'm a private man, don't much like folk. Don't like 'em knowin' nothin' I don't tell 'em myself. Ya understand?"

Where he's going with this? "Yes, Boss."

"Billy had no right to talkin' 'bout me. Guess that's why I took it bad when ya told me things I ain't told ya myself. I was mad, but I ain't mad no more." He shifts again. "I'm not a feelin' man, unless you count my temper." His eyes find mine, soft as I ever seen 'em. "You got feelin's?"

My heart's fit to burst with 'em. "Yes, Boss."

"All right." He paused, as though what he wanted to say had to break through. "Yer the closest thing to a friend I ever had, and that means I got feelin's 'bout what passes between us."

"I—uh—thank you?"

"*Thank you.* That all ya got to say?"

"I wasn't expecting it, is all."

"But d'ya care? 'Bout what passes between us?"

I'm frightened what he's saying is gonna make sleeping all kinds of tough. "Yes, Boss."

He pushes himself up to sitting. "Help me get dressed."

"But why?"

"I'm fixin' to sit with ya over dinner." He coughs, winces. "If ya'll have me."

Dressing him in his long johns is hard—he's still weak and heavy in his arms and legs—but I manage it in time.

Getting him back to the dinner table takes as long as it did to get him to his room, and although he's sitting at the table, he's leaning on it and breathing deep.

I place his meal in front of him, then sit opposite.

I close my eyes to pray, and he lets me do it without interrupting. Not that he ever interrupts me, but the '*God, God, God*' is stinging me enough to think he might. When I'm done saying grace inside my head, I eat, and he does the same.

He doesn't use a knife. Instead, he digs through the meat with the edge of his fork. "It's good."

"Thank you, Boss."

His eating slows, then he puts down his fork and stares at the rim of his plate. "Ya can use my name if ya like."

His words rob me of a heartbeat and cold runs down my back as though the snow outside's found its way down my collar. "Is that proper?"

"Does yer storybook say different?"

"No, but—"

"Then it's fine. Use my name."

Marius Tillman. "Is Tillman good?"

A smile plays on Tillman's lips. "Good enough. Ya got a surname?"

"It's Noble, Boss."

"Told ya to call me Tillman."

"Right. It's Noble, Tillman."

"Well, I can't be callin' ya *Noble* all the time. It'll go to ya head. I'll call ya by yer first name, *Faron*."

My name on his lips splits my mouth into a smile.

Tillman smiles back. "I work the spread and ya take care of the place ... and me." He pauses.

"We're a team, friends is sumthin' we'll work on. Deal?"

"Thank you, Tillman. Means a lot."

"Ain't never had a friend, have ya?"

"Guess not."

"Me neither, but I'll do my best. Can't promise I'll keep my temper in check, but I'll do what I can." He grins down at his food, then gets to finishing it.

My mind's racing. Will being friends light a fire under the feelings I've been avoiding? Will it need praying on? I catch up with finishing my food, then clear the table.

"I'd help," Tillman says, "but I'd probably drop it seein' as I'm weak as a kitten."

I put the plates and eating irons in the kitchen sink. "Ain't no bother," I call out. "I'm used to doing it myself."

"That ya are," Tillman says. "We got anythin' sweet to eat, Faron? Sumthin' sweet'll make me feel better."

Faron. Will I ever get over the jolting when he says it? I go back to the table.

Tillman's leaning forward, but now he's got his hands folded under his chin. "I seem to remember sumthin' about a pie." Grunting, Tillman places his hands, palms down, on the table. "What do you say, Faron? Reckon we should take a bite of sumthin' sweet?"

I sit on the edge of the dinner table. "That's why I made it."

Tillman's eyes glaze over as though he's dreaming. "Sumthin' sweet's a comfort on a cold night." He folds his arms behind his head, then sits back. His face twists. "Jesus!"

I lean forward, grab his long johns, then pull him forward. "You gotta be careful. Those stitches are fresh."

"All right. All right." He's sweating again. "Weren't thinkin' straight is all."

Me neither, and that's the problem. "I'll get you something for the pain."

Tillman waves a hand at me. "That damn tea? With herbs? Save it for sumthin' better."

He's too stubborn for his own good. "Like losing a limb?" I say. "I'm making it."

He laughs a little. "You're stubborn."

"And you're not?"

A few minutes later, I'm handing him a cup of herbal tea. "Drink it."

Tillman sips, but real slow, like it might be poison. He looks at me from under his lashes. "This gonna help me sleep?"

"Uh-huh."

"Good," he says. "Need some rest. Pain's awful tirin'."

Getting Tillman to his room's easier than before because now he's taking some of his weight. Once we're by the bed, I move my hands to the buttons on his long johns. The silence is back, thicker than the snow outside. I fumble with a button, but Tillman closes his hands over mine.

"Leave it to me," he says, real soft.

I frown at him. "Ain't nothing I haven't seen before, remember?"

"Not so sure 'bout that." Tillman nudges my hands away. "Help me onto the bed. I'll sleep in these."

I lay him down, then go to the curtains.

"Leave 'em open," Tillman says. "Sky's clear. I'll take pleasure in seein' the stars before that tea knocks me out."

"All right," I say, turning out his lamp. "Good night, Tillman."

Smiling softly, he looks up at me. "G'night Faron. Sleep well, ya hear?"

"That I will."

Leaving him to his stargazing, I get to washing up. I'd seen him naked before, so why his sudden modesty? What meaning should I take from that?

I finish the dishes, then put 'em away.

In my room, I undress, climb into bed, then take my Bible from the nightstand. Turning the pages, I pray for God's guidance in finding a passage that speaks to me.

I think I find one.

> No temptation has overtaken you that is not common to man.
>
> — 1 CORINTHIANS 10:13

But I find no comfort in the words. All I get from it is that Tillman can be tempted too, then we'll both be overtaken by it.

Will I ever sleep again?

The next morning, Tillman's still fast asleep, and

I'm drinking strong black coffee and looking at his wife's picture, thinking on how things'd be different if she'd lived. How many kids would they have had by now? Would they look like him or her? *I sure as hell wouldn't have been here.*

I haul on two jackets, then leave the cabin to give the horses their morning feed.

Outside is blinding—a blazing sun in a clear sky beating down on snow, turning it whiter than I ever saw. I shield my eyes, letting 'em adjust, then take in the ... nothing, like my eyes have stopped seeing, forgotten how to see. Slowly, I make out a few shapes, but they're all covered in the cold stuff.

It has to be fifty below and the cold takes my breath away, tasting like a metal that can burn you. There's a blizzard in the distance, looking like smoke, only moving so fast, I know it'll be on us soon. If I can get the horses fed and my ass back inside before it hits, I'll be a lucky man.

It snowed overnight, sixteen inches in as many hours, and getting to the barn's a bitch, like I'm in some strange maze. The world is white, no horizon, no shadows, no colour, just blinding white.

I make it to the barn, dig away enough snow to wrench the broken barn door open, then I stop.

There's a sound like the ice's growling at me.

To my left, hot breath steams in the air. I don't see the wolf, but I don't have to. I sense it. I sense it as it darts at me, its teeth bared, jaws open. I leap to the right, raising my arms. The wolf's teeth sink into my jacket sleeve, but not my skin. I throw myself against it, and we both slide in the snow. I grab its snout, twisting it sideways, and pin the wolf down. It thrashes beneath me, but I'm too strong, too determined. I refuse to let go, to let it win.

The blizzard's closing in, but all that matters is this fight and right now, I got the upper hand. Deep down, there's a wild hunger rising up—an urge to win this fight and prove that there ain't nothing stronger than the will of a man when he puts his mind to something.

We roll around in the snow, locked in a struggle. The wolf tries to shake me off, but I'm not letting go. With all the strength I can muster, I shove it away from me, then scramble to my feet.

I stare down at that wild animal as it slowly rises, its eyes blazing with hate. For a moment we stand there facing each other, our chests heaving from effort, and then the blizzard hits us both.

The wind lashes at my face as snow swirls around us in chaos. But I don't look away from that wolf. Not for one second do I turn my back on it as I take one step backward, then a second, then a third.

The wolf watches me the whole time, its eyes never leaving mine.

Then I see it. I see Tillman's dead wife reflected in the wolf's eyes. I keep taking steps backward, and it keeps coming forward, step after step. Was this the same wolf that took her from him? The same one that's coming for me?

Its eyes burn into mine, damning me. Or is it her damning me? Is she the wolf? No, it can't be. It's just a crazy thought.

We stay like that until finally the whiteout eats us both up, and I can't see it no more. But I know it's still there, waiting for its chance to come at me again.

I don't know how many steps I take until my heel strikes something hard, and I lose my balance, crashing back.

Then the wolf's coming, coming fast, leaping onto my chest and sending a spray of snow into my eyes.

Yelling, I shove at it, but the blizzard steals my voice. The snow's blinding me, making it hard to see, but I know the wolf's bared its teeth. *I can't let it get me.*

I can't let it get me.

I can't.

I scream.

Then there's a shot, a flash of red, and the wolf wheels away.

Looking up, I see the barrel of a gun and Tillman holding it.

"Ya'll right?" he shouts, his words almost lost in the thick, silver air. The blizzard's eating them up, stifling the air until it's like breathing cotton.

My chest is pumping, but I nod all the same. I feel like I'm going to puke or pass out or both.

"S'all right," Tillman says. "It's over."

"Think there's more?" I say, scrambling back until my back's against his legs.

His jaw sets tight. "Damn right."

Grabbing my arm, Tiliman pulls me up the stairs toward the cabin.

I can't feel my feet from the cold, but I ain't falling on my face. "What're you doing?" I say.

"Gettin' ya inside, ya damn fool."

"No, I gotta feed the horses—we're gonna lose 'em."

"Don't be worryin' 'bout them," he says, yanking the door open. "Get inside. Now."

"But," I say, but then the cold slams into me again, rattling my teeth.

"No buts, Faron. You're gonna turn into an icicle out here. Now move."

The cabin draws me back into reality, nudging its warmth up my sleeves and down my collar. I'm standing on the floor of the parlour, but Tillman's got me by the arms, pushing me toward the fire, bringing me face to face with his wife.

Keeping my eyes away from hers, I shuck off my jackets, checking the spot where the wolf bit. My forearm's red and a little swollen.

"Gonna bruise," Tillman says, voice flat, putting his gun by the door.

Silence settles over the cabin, and I don't know if it's the blizzard or something else.

What's he thinking? What am I thinking?

"You all right?" I say, my eyes searching his.

"Me? Why're ya lookin' at me? I ain't the one who got bit."

"You were outside, too."

"Inside for most of it," he says, his eyebrows scrunching together.

"Hell of a shot," I say, my eyes drifting toward the gun by the door.

"Yeah, well …" His eyes flick toward the back of the cabin, then the front, staying away from mine.

Whatever it is he's thinking, he doesn't want me to know.

"What?" I say, stepping toward him, testing him. "What is it?"

"Don't rightly know," he says. "The wolf …" Tillman stares at his dead wife's photograph like he's turned to stone. "Ya did real good. Proud of ya."

A wolf took her, you fool. Of course he's thinking about her.

He just keeps staring at her picture.

Say something, dumbass. "I think she'd have been proud of you. You know, for saving me out there."

He finally looks at me, and his eyes are wet. "Much obliged to ya, Faron." And then he does something I never would've expected: He hugs me.

I lean into him, and if this is it, if this is all I'm getting, I don't want to let go.

"Come on, let's get you warmed up." He walks me closer to the fire. "What Billy told ya," he says, suddenly letting me go, "'bout my wife? Weren't true. She didn't die."

"She didn't?"

"She left me."

I couldn't leave him, and I couldn't imagine ever wanting to, either. "But why?"

Grinding his jaw, he turns away from me. "Because I didn't have no interest in her, ya know?" he says, his voice fading to a whisper. "The way a man should be interested in a woman." He puts his hand on the mantle, dips his head like he's tired, then curls his other hand into a fist. "First she reckoned sumthin' was wrong with her, then she figured it was me."

"I guess people fall for the wrong people. Sometimes."

"She left me for another man."

At a loss for anything else, all I can give him is, "I'm sorry."

He shrugs. "Don't be. She found a man who gives her what she needs."

"And you?" I ask, kind of quiet.

He turns to me, and for the first time, I see defeat in him. "Reckon I found that too."

Confused, I blink. "Me?"

"I mean, she was prettier than you," he says, his lips twitching, but his face sets grim when I don't laugh.

I open my mouth to speak, to tell him I can't

believe what he's saying, but he raises a hand to shush me.

"Can't nothin' come of it," he says quickly, his gaze fixed on the floor. "You're a God-fearin' man, and I wouldn't blame ya for running straight out that door, wolf or no wolf."

But I'm rooted to the spot and can't go anywhere, even if I want to. My legs won't work. I can't even breathe.

Tillman rocks on his heels as though he wants to take off himself. "She made me a deal—let her go with her beau and she wouldn't tell no one."

"Where'd they go?"

"A ways away. Heard talk of Utah." He makes to step towards me, then stops. "All I ask, Faron, is that this stays between us. Will ya do that one thing? Not tell a soul 'bout what I said, what I am?"

"I won't," I say.

We stare at each other for a moment, and then he nods and turns back to the picture. He's quiet and I'm quiet, too, because I don't know what to say. Do I tell him it's all right? Do I tell him I don't care?

His hand on the mantle twitches.

I don't want to leave, but I can't keep going the way I've been going, pretending I don't have feelings for the man. I feel like Tillman wants me to say something, like I need to say something, but I'm afraid to say anything at all. So I just stand there.

I look at his wife's picture, and I see something I hadn't noticed before. Her hands lay in her lap, her hair is pulled back, and her lips are set in a smile that looks like she's hoping for something good.

Just like me.

I reach out, then touch her face. I don't know why I'm doing it, don't know why I feel the need, but I do. It makes me feel closer to her, to Tillman.

Taking the picture of his wife, Tillman crouches down, then makes to put it on the fire.

"What are you doing?" I say, putting a hand on his shoulder.

His jaw's tight. "Burnin' her."

"No," I say. "She was good people. She's deserving of better."

"And she got better." He's standing again, looking around like he's not sure what to do with the picture.

I take it from him and put it on the table.

No temptation has overtaken you that is not common to man. God is faithful, and he will not let you be tempted beyond your ability, but

> with the temptation he will also provide the way of escape, that you may be able to endure it.
>
> — 1 CORINTHIANS 10:13

This is it. This is my temptation. And it's Tillman's too. And we can't escape it or the storm outside, the storm *inside*.

"I want to stay," I say, my voice shaking. I go to take a step forward, but I freeze like I'm still outside. "I had feelings for a long time but was too ashamed to admit 'em."

We're staring at each other, and Tillman looks like he's not sure what to do.

"So, are you asking me?" I say. "Are you asking me to stay?"

Tillman grinds his jaw, and I think he's about to say something about it being a sin, that it can't ever happen, but he doesn't. He just looks nervous. "Reckon I am."

I step close to him, not knowing if it's the fire or his closeness that's filling me with warmth. "Then I reckon I'll stay."

We stare at each other for a moment before

Tillman nods and steps back. It's like he's relieved, but he's also trying to hide it.

"Glad," he says, his voice low and strained. "Glad you're stayin'."

He glances back at his wife's picture, and I see a smile play at the corner of his mouth. A smile that's understanding, forgiving, and maybe even hoping for something good, too.

"What are you thinking about?" I say, wondering if I'll ever get used to the spark of joy at seeing him smile.

"Reckon the world's been turned upside down," he says, ducking his head like he's coming over shy. "Reckon I ain't never been happier in my whole life."

He looks at me, and I look at him, and who knows how long we'll have to wait for the storm to pass.

"What about ya?" he whispers. "How do ya feel?"

"Like I've spent my whole life waiting for this moment."

"Yeah?" he says, his voice cracking. "Likewise."

He wraps his arms around me, pulls me into him, and I bury my face in his shoulder. He smells like smoke and gunpowder, but it's a good smell.

This is a good smell.

"Tillman?"

"Yeah?" he says, his voice warm in my ear.

"It's been here, inside me, for a long time. I ain't never felt another emotion so strong."

"Me neither." He rests his chin on the top of my head. "We'll figure it out."

"Ain't never been more afraid of anything in my life."

"Don't be," he says, his voice softer than it's ever been. "We got each other."

"Yeah," I say, squeezing him back. "We got each other."

Out here. Out here in the cold.

THE SIREN'S PHOTOGRAPH

TAYLOR MCLEOD

The Grand Hall rose around her as she stood under the rotunda. The white marble floor and walls reflected the sunlight streaming in through the windows and made the whole place seem as though it was on fire. The evening sun danced around the hall in flashes of red and gold. Had this been any other occasion then Lady Avaya would have found it quite a beautiful sight.

She stood in the middle of the hall, her blood-stained dress seeming to sparkle amongst all the marble. Around the sides of the hall were the lesser Lords and Ladies, all dressed as if they were attending some magical event. They stared at her with beady and hungry eyes. They had expected a spectacle, but a massacre like this was a surprise to them. Not a bad surprise though. It would keep the gossip alive in this city for months. That was good enough for them.

The High Lord of Lamba, Sir Edmund Kew, sat on this throne and surveyed the hall. He looked at Lady Avaya with casual disinterest as he contemplated his opening speech. Around the edge of the hall, there was the usual crowd of lesser Lords and Ladies of the city. Each of them was dressed in the finest clothing, their wrists and necks dripping in jewels that Lady Avaya did not even know the names of. Despite her time as a captive of this city, she still found their customs and their whole way of life completely bizarre. Each of the lesser Lords and Ladies seemed to be ignoring her completely though as their eyes were all transfixed on their beloved Sir Edmund.

"I don't know why you did it." Sir Edmund now spoke. He looked at Avaya with a mix of confusion and disgust as he continued with his speech. "My son gave you everything you didn't have. He took you from that silly little village and made you into a real Lady. He even married you! Why would you betray him the way you did?"

"Your son kidnapped me from my home. He took

me against my will, kept me in a cage in his chambers and used me as a plaything." Lady Avaya spoke as coolly as she could. Sir Edmund as a person was not a threat, but as an authority figure he could have her killed with one wave of his hand. Lady Avaya glanced momentarily at the guards posted throughout the hall. They were huge, bulky machines that the preceding High Lords of Lamba had created to 'keep the peace'. They were broad, tall, and obscenely intimidating. They were twice the size of a normal man and fitted with so much extra technology that they were no more than an animatronic in a skin suit. Built to obey, they were arguably less human than even the sirens that this city so loved to fear. Sir Edmund used these guards as his own personal army and hired killers. They got their hands dirty so Sir Edmund could continue to adorn his hands in fine jewels and keep his position as the High Lord of Lamba.

"But surely that was still a better life than the one you had in your village." Sir Edmund sighed.

"You saw the memory replay-" Avaya began.

"Yes yes, we all saw the memory replay." Sir Edmund waved his hand impatiently. "But how do I know it is real?"

"Excuse me?" Avaya was confused by this

comment. The whole reason memories were downloaded for viewing was because they could not be altered. The memory chips every person had embedded in their brain was no more than a live camera feed that captured everything as it happened. The whole point of having them was so that there could be no argument over what happened in any given situation.

"How do I know you didn't tamper with it in some way?"

"How could I have done that?"

"You tell me. You are practically one of those sirens after all. Aren't all of you village savages part siren?"

"Well..." Avaya thought about her response for a moment. Technically they were all 'part siren'. Anyone in this room had the potential to become a siren. The only issue was that making a siren had been outlawed at least five generations ago. "Is it not illegal to make a siren?"

"Oh, here we go." Again, Sir Edmund sighed. "Again with your villager views. Everyone knows that a siren can be made through poor technology, and I imagine in your tiny villages the only technology you have is poor technology."

"Sirens were made by replacing human bodies bit by bit with technology and-"

"Shut up with your stupid, braindead thoughts!" Sir Edmund leant forward in his chair clearly getting annoyed that he was having to have this conversation. Even though this entire trial had been his own idea. He could have left her in the prison cell to rot away but he was the one who wanted to make a scene of it all. To make an example of her. The lowly villager who had killed his son. "The matter at hand is that you killed my son. This city's beloved Sir Jaxon. He rescued you and you murdered him in cold blood."

"He was going to kill me!" Lady Avaya tried to defend herself. "You saw the memory. You saw him beat me and then try to strangle me."

"And yet I have already established that you faked that memory. You altered it with your siren ways!" Sir Edmund shouted back.

"I am not a siren!" Lady Avaya protested. A ripple went around the room as the words traveled through each member. They all stood there hungry for the next fierce exchange of words.

"Prove it." Sir Edmund said bluntly.

"How?"

"If you are indeed not a siren, then there is one

way to prove it." He leant forward in his throne and a twisted smile appeared across his face. "Go to one of their dens." There was an excited buzz of electricity passing through the crowd of spectators, which soon became heavy with anticipation for how Avaya would respond.

"That's suicide." Lady Avaya responded quietly. But Sir Edmund already knew this. Either way he had her cornered. If she approached the den, she would most likely be killed by the notoriously territorial siren alpha, but if she lived it would simply prove to him that she was in fact a siren. Either way, she would most likely be killed.

"I thought you wild people knew how to handle sirens?" Sir Edmund mocked her.

"We know how to co-exist." Lady Avaya responded bluntly. "But that does not mean the sirens won't attack us if they feel threatened."

"If you long for your prison of village life so much, how about we make a deal instead?" Sir Edmund flashed another twisted smile at her. Avaya felt a chill go through her body as his eyes seemed to bore through her.

"What kind of deal?"

"You know, no one has ever seen a siren up close." Sir Edmund rose from his throne now and slowly walked towards Avaya in the center of the room. "No one has ever gotten close enough to find out what they really look like. None of our people would be so stupid." A small laugh left his mouth, which inevitably sent the crowd of spectators into a fit of giggles as well. "But you would know how to get close enough without being spotted. You could sneak past their defenses."

"Why would you want me to do that?" His information was not fully correct. Sirens did not have defenses like these cities had defenses. The sirens had defenses in the same way that wild animals had defenses.

"I would like a photograph of the siren alpha." Sir Edmund was now stood before Avaya. He had broad shoulders and thick arms, but years of being dotted on hand and foot had caused his mass to become fluffy. No doubt he was strong, and, in many situations, he could be quite the imposing warrior, but here in this marbled castle he was no more than a rich man. All his strength now came from the guards that shadowed him and the power that had been passed down to him in a title. His son had been no different and Lady Avaya had managed to overpower him in the end.

"A photograph?" Avaya repeated, somewhat

confused. Sir Edmund simply nodded his head slowly in response. He grinned down at her.

"That is all you want me to get. A photograph of just one siren?"

"The alpha siren, yes. That is all I require." Sir Edmund rocked slightly on his feet, as though this was a casual conversation and not the death sentence Avaya knew it to be. His smile did not falter. A quick sparkle of light glistened in his eyes, suggesting that this was not actually all that he would require.

"And by photograph you mean..." Avaya tried to search Sir Edmund's face but all she could see was that smile.

"I mean a photograph." He giggled to himself, as if this explanation was giving away some big secret or a juicy piece of gossip. "You point the camera and click." A hum of more giggling echoed around the room as the spectators joined in with the revelry.

"Will you provide me with the camera?" Avaya asked.

"Of course."

"And supplies?"

"Of course." He shrugged his shoulders as though this was an obvious response.

"And then you'll release me?"

"If you get me the photo that I want."

"And if I get this photograph for you, you'll allow me to leave this city in peace. To return to my village in peace." Lady Avaya set out her terms of this agreement.

"But of course."

"And you won't come near my village or the lands surrounding it ever again."

"Agreed. You have my word as a just ruler." Sir Edmund sarcastically placed a chubby, ring laden hand across his chest. Avaya wanted to believe him but there was something all too ironic in that sentence.

"Is there a deadline?" Avaya asked eventually.

"Nope." He responded simply.

"Moving or still image?"

"I have not decided yet. Make it both." There it was. There was the sneaky part to his plan. A still photo could be taken with no issues, at a safe distance away and without alerting the sirens to her presence. But a moving photo would require a degree of intimacy Avaya was not certain she could achieve. Not with a siren and most certainly not with the alpha. Strictly speaking though this would not be a photo at all then.

"Very well." Avaya bowed her head slightly. This

was the closest to a curtsy that these city High Lords would ever get from her, despite their years of trying to beat it into her. She turned and walked out of the grand hall, the blood of her dress reflecting off the marble as she strode forward and tried to ignore the snickering and the whispers of the lesser Lords and Ladies.

"Do you want to know why I want the photo?" Sir Edmund's voice echoed around the hall.

"That is not my business." Avaya stopped but did not turn around. She knew what he wanted with the photo. Everyone knew why he wanted this photo. Everyone knew about his hobby. Yet to say it out loud would make it seem too real. Too barbaric and too crass. But Sir Edmund knew this. That was why he wanted it discussed. He wanted to see Avaya cringe at the thought of it and to see her twist in disgust as the explanation moved across her lips before tainting the marble walls that sheltered them as she uttered them aloud.

"Shall I explain it to you?" His voice was mocking now. Not just mocking Avaya though but mocking every other Lord and Lady in the room that had up until this moment clung to every word he uttered. Now they shrank back against the cold marble walls. They all knew what he would say.

They had all heard the rumors of what he did to his collection of photos. How he would manipulate the pixels and rewrite the code to bring the photograph to life in his own hologram hell. Being a siren was considered to be a fate worse than death, but to be one of his holograms would mean an eternity of suffering. Lady Avaya turned to look over her shoulder, seeing the High Lord's smirk even from this distance.

"Should I tell you how a hologram feels?" He asked again, his smirk intensifying. A shiver went around the room. The lesser Lords and Ladies tried to remain composed, but Avaya saw a few flinches as his words echoed through the hall.

"Only if I can tell you how it felt killing your son." Avaya replied coolly. His smirk vanished immediately, and Avaya could feel the hatred of his eyes burn through her. But she held his gaze and tried to ignore the ripple that was going through the room. Sir Jaxon had been much loved, but they loved the gossip more. The memory they had all had to see had shook their very understanding of who Sir Jaxon had been behind closed doors. Now they were all eager for more. Sir Edmund opened his mouth to say something but simply waved his hand at her. Avaya turned to face the doorway and held her head high as the guards opened the heavy doors for her to leave.

Surprisingly Sir Edmund was true to his word. She was given a list of places to visit, where she would be able to collect the various items she would need for her journey. At the armory she was given a small but heavy bag that had a large hammer, an EMP mine and a phone inside it. The phone was arguably the only thing that would come in handy. The store assistant who handed her the bag looked at her apologetically, as if this worker had any say in what the bag contained.

"I'm sorry." The store assistant offered in a meek voice. "So not fair. I always thought at least these Lords all seem like a bunch of weirdos." Avaya smiled politely and thanked them for their help. She hated the sympathy. She knew they couldn't help it, that their sympathy was something innate to them. But she hated it all the same. She wasn't sure what was worse though. The people who glared and jeered at her as she walked through the hallways or the people who whispered condolences with sad eyes as she walked past them. Both acted like they had any idea what she had been through. What had been taken from her. What she had been forced to do to survive her time as a prisoner in their adored city. They knew nothing, but a small part of her hoped that no one else would ever know how she felt right now.

Avaya flung the bag over her shoulder and headed to the main market. She walked into the wide-open courtyard and tried not to notice the strange silence that descended as she walked over to the various stalls.

The owner of the charging station was the least hospitable, but she carried the most important items that Avaya would need for her journey. Technological advances meant food and water were rarely needed, however all technology needed to be charged and, in the wilderness, sleep was not always an option. The charging packs would therefore keep her awake and moving without having to risk sleeping in the elements. The owner of the stall looked older than she was, and her mouth was constantly pursed as if she was sucking on something sour. Her name was Lizbeth and despite her somewhat humble appearance as a shop owner, she was a devout follower. Avaya had seen her many a time following Sir Jaxon, as if being in close proximity to the ruling elite would somehow brush off onto her. Maybe she thought that if she appeared in front of Sir Jaxon's path enough times that he would invite her to stay with him. Yet every time he pushed her aside, she would still try again the next day. Avaya would have felt sorry for her if Lizbeth wasn't such a horrid person on her own merit.

Avaya asked her four times for the items that had been put aside for her as Lizbeth pretended not to see or hear her, instead busing herself with something on her phone or with the gaming app she had implanted in her arm. Lizbeth only paid attention when Avaya, having grown frustrated with the rudeness, reached across the stall counter to grab the bundle of goods that were wrapped in a piece of cloth that was clearly stamped with the High Lord's sigil across it.

"Filthy savage." Lizbeth spat across the table as she snatched the bundle of goods out of Avaya's hands.

"Those were put aside for me." Avaya tried to speak calmly. This was how every one of their interactions went and so some of Lizbeth's hatred had been dulled over the years.

"Why are we even helping you? Do you know how many people in this city are having to power their homes with push bike generators?" She stood holding the bundle close to her chest. Avaya momentarily felt sorry for her. This woman should have been one of the richest in the city, because she carried one of the most prized goods. Yet she clearly wasn't despite her very many years of trying. Her clothes were high quality but were also starting to noticeably discolor from years of wear and tear. Her hair was thin and as Avaya watched, a small glitch went across the haggard face as she stood there glaring at Avaya.

"Your Lord has said-"

"Well, you savages are basically sirens anyway, aren't you?" Avaya immediately stopped feeling sorry for this lady. For the city as a whole. The ignorant and outdated views spewed through by Sir Edmund spread through the city like a virus. She would happily take every resource they had. Let them pedal themselves to death just to keep the lights on. Cities like these did more harm than good in her opinion and her time spent here had only reinforced that belief.

"We arc actually-" Avaya tried to explain the difference between the two yet again but was immediately cut off.

"You're all the bloody same." Lizbeth now leant forward, and the smell of fried electrics emanated from her. This was a sure sign that a tooth implant had short circuited. Or perhaps a thyroid implant had contracted a bit of a virus and the organic organ was now working overtime to remove the artificial implant. That would explain why she seemed to be out of breath despite the fact she had barely moved an inch. "You village people and those sirens are all the same. You're all working together, aren't you? I bet it was all a plan for you to come here and kill our Lord."

"Your Lord was a forty-year-old man who kidnapped me from my home, took me as his personal slave and was then forced to marry me to avoid a massive political scandal." Avaya replied bluntly.

"You ungrateful-" Lizbeth's face twisted in disgust. Avaya always found it funny how in the cities, the people had ideas of the world that never matched with reality. Avaya had not lied and yet Lizbeth was acting like it was a personal attack on her own honor.

"Were you there?" Avaya asked plainly. "Were you there when your Lord burned down half of my village? Were you there when he beat me unconscious, took me back to this city of his and used me as his personal punching bag?"

"All lies!"

"Your Lord was a massive psychopath. He was more unhinged than the sirens."

"And you thought that meant he had to die?" Lizbeth backed away slightly, still clutching the bundle as if it was all that kept her upright. "I thought you villagers loved the ferocity of the sirens?"

"My villagers knew how to live in peace with the sirens. Your Lord did not know how to live in peace with anyone or anything."

"So you're glad he died?" The question hung in the air for a moment. Was Avaya glad that Sir Jaxon was dead? She was glad the torture was at an end. No matter what awaited her out in the wilderness it would feel like pleasure compared to what her captor had put her through. But she had never taken any life before. The look on his face when the knife sank into his neck would be forever burned into her memory. She had not wanted to kill him, but with his hands around her throat she had done what she had to. She had reached out for whatever she could find and that just happened to be the hilt of his own dagger.

"I sense disagreement. What is the situation?" A guard appeared next to Avaya. He loomed over both women and Avaya was relieved to see Lizbeth shrink slightly in fear of this machine.

"The Killer Bride here wants goods." Lizbeth said finally with a pout. Avaya flinched briefly at the use of that name. She had heard it muttered as she walked through the city but to hear it said out loud felt wrong. Her skin itched with the venom the name carried. In her village she dreamt of one day being called a bride, but now the word seemed tainted to her. It sounded worse to her now than the label of a killer. She would one day come to terms with this part of herself but being his bride had offended every part of her being.

"The High Lord has requested certain items be made available to her." The guard wouldn't even say her name. It was either an insult or - as Avaya largely suspected - the guards had never been told her name because Sir Edmund himself never bothered to learn it properly. Who was she compared to the High Families? Her name was as meaningless to him as her life had been to his son.

"But-"

"Do you defy the High Lord of Lamba?" The guard turned to look at Lizbeth now and Avaya could hear the soft whirring noise of his internal system as he carried out a full background check. No doubt he was scanning the very many electronic chips throughout her body and looking for anything that would warrant an arrest. Even just an outdated chip part would suffice.

"No." Lizbeth sounded panicked now. "No issues here Sir. I just meant that..." She stumbled over the words slightly as she opened the bundle and pretended to fuss with the contents.

"The High Lord has requested certain items be made available to her."

"Yes, and here they are." She forced a smile and clumsily rebound the goods. "All you need to get there and back. If you come back." She held out the bundle for Avaya to take. Avaya reached for it. Lizbeth however dropped the bundle over the counter and onto the floor, where the lazy knot that she had used to tie the fabric together came undone. Lizbeth and the guard watched as the contents clattered onto the concrete ground and Avaya had to stoop to collect it all. From the ground, she saw the subtle smile of satisfaction across Lizbeth's face.

"You are to head to the front gate for final inspection." The guard said as Avaya knelt on the ground, shoving the items into her bag. She stood but left the piece of cloth on the floor.

"Thank you for your assistance." Avaya nodded

her head slightly to the lady, who looked at her angrily once more. Avaya knew better than to cause a scene in front of a guard. She had seen all too often what happened to people - from the commoners to the Lords and Ladies themselves - who disobeyed a guard.

She stood and followed the guard out of the courtyard and towards the back gates. The city was enclosed by two layers of wall. The inside wall was brick and concrete. Somewhat archaic but it had been standing here since the city was first built, long before any sort of power surge or grid blackout. The outside wall was made of thick steel. Avaya had first thought that the steel was used to help boost the solar panels collection of sunshine, especially during the sweltering summer months so that their energy stores would last them throughout the darker and wetter winter months. But when she was captured and was being dragged back towards Lamba behind the Little Lord's horse, the reflection from the steel sheets nearly blinded her. It acted to confuse people, playing with the lights and near blinding travelers so that they could not get their bearings correctly. With the lights reflected at a blinding intensity it was hard to gauge how far away the city really was.

Avaya stood by the first set of reinforced doors that led to the wasteland outside. An army of guards were posted here on the ground, with another small army positioned day and night upon the top to deal with any potential threats. Sometimes as Avaya had laid in her cage at night, nursing her new wounds, she could hear EMPs and electrical beacons firing outside the walls. The guards doing what they were made to do.

Avaya was escorted through the first set of doors and then the second by four of the hulking guards. They walked beside her in a box formation and escorted her outside into the wasteland. The sun was high and as Avaya looked around her, she could see nothing, but barren fields and the odd broken down house. The guards walked in synchronization and due to their extreme height and gait Avaya found herself having to jog slightly to keep up with them. Every time she slowed down slightly to be in line with the two guards behind her, both guards would reach out one hand and poke her roughly with one sausage sized finger. It would send a sharp electric shock through her body and was a very clear warning to keep moving forward.

After about five hundred meters, the guards stopped. In a quick movement, the guards in front turned to look down at her, and all four guards aimed their open hands at her, the blasters in their palms glowing a faint red as they showed that their weapons were armed and ready to fire. She did not need a second invitation and briskly walked between the two front guards. She glanced back when she thought she had enough distance and saw all four of them stood in a single line, their hands still raised ready to fire should she truly lose her mind and attempt to go back to the city.

The route was simple enough, but the terrain would be treacherous and unpredictable. The siren she was to take a photo of was likely to be very territorial, to the point where even the High Lord's own army could not get past the defenses. But Lady Avaya had been brought up knowing how to recognise and deal with the sirens. Living in a village left her with no choice. The rural areas were the perfect place for siren nesting grounds, away from the noise and electricity of the big cities that could cause too many power surges or glitches to the sirens.

Once outside of the city boundaries, the wasteland spread out before her like an empty canvas. The once paved roads were broken and discolored from the acid rain and powerful sandstorms that battered this part of the kingdom. Broken houses lined the roads on either side, but no noise could be heard but for the howling, grieving wind that blew the smell of rust and decay across her face. Each step kicked up more of the scorched earth that added the smell of sulfur and burning to the air. Every breath she took tasted sour and metallic. Whatever this area had been before was now no more than target practice for the guards or hunting grounds for the Lords and Ladies who needed adrenaline. The animal carcasses abandoned beside some of the houses was evidence that a hunt had taken place not long ago, their decaying bodies left to the elements. Hunting was no longer a necessity. It was just for the cruelty of it. The only light that could be seen was from the pylons that flickered along the streets, dotted between the houses to remind everyone of an era long since forgotten.

She held up her phone and a small map appeared on the screen. She followed the augmented reality lines across the street, her phone showing which roads to turn down, and which houses had high electrical readings. This suggested either inhabitants or faulty electrics. Either way Avaya knew to keep her distance from them. As the daylight drew dimmer, the howling wind began to pick up around her until she could barely see where the lines were leading her due to the amount of ash and grit that was being whipped up. Occasionally the noise of creaking floorboards or a slipping tile could be heard emanating from one of the dilapidated houses would cause her to flip her head in the direction of the sound, watching for any sign of movement in the broken windows while shielding her eyes from the harsh wind. She could not feel any eyes watching her, but Avaya knew to keep moving forward. To make it clear that she had no reason to harm whatever inhabitants this broken town still had, nor that she had any business with them.

The sirens' main place of residence - where they had set up the den for their colony - was at the end of a side road, based in what appeared to be an old town house. An old information sign hung askew on its post, suggesting that before the blackouts and the power surges this property had been a town museum. A small sliver of green light was scratched across the front of this sign, and it began to blink rhythmically as Avaya drew nearer. This was a sure sign that sirens were nearby. She had been taught from a young age in her village to recognise what was a siren track and what was just faulty electrics.

As she walked past the sign and closer to the building, multiple voices sounded through her head. They sounded like an echo that floated through her mind. Avaya stopped, trying to determine whether the sound was real or imagined, as if the wind was trying to play games with her.

"Come no closer." The voices sounded like several people were whispering in her ear. She spun around quickly but there was nothing around her. She had heard stories of the sirens communicating like this, using the technology in people's bodies to make it seem that their words were a person's own thoughts. It felt far less intrusive than she had imagined it would do. Somehow it felt...comforting. To know that despite the decay and ruin around her she was at least not alone.

"I do not come of free will." She responded. She lowered her bag onto the ground and knelt silently in the empty road. Ahead of her, multiple figures emerged from the property and the surrounding houses and were slowly walking towards her. Avaya did not dare move her head to look but she was certain she could feel figures appearing behind her as well.

"Then why are you here?" The collective voices grated on her ears, leaving invisible scratches with every syllable spoken. She bowed her head and raised the phone in front of her in the palm of her hand as an offering. She had always been taught to avoid eye contact with a siren as they could take it as a sign of aggression. So she bent her head to look at the ground, leaning her head slightly against the wind to avoid more grit getting into her eyes or her mouth.

"I was sent here by the High Lord of Lamba to take your picture. It is the only way I will be released from his prison." Avaya felt no need to lie or make up a story. Sirens had been human once, and despite their extensive augmentations their human brains were still largely intact.

"So, he has sent you to me." One of the figures spoke out loud now, sounding as if it was smiling. Their voice sounded organic, with only the slightest hint of autotuning. It sounded patient and calm but then that was how it had been designed to be. "The disgraced Lady Avaya. The Killer Bride." Even with the beating wind against her, she could feel the ripple of excitement go through the crowd of figures.

"It is not a name I am proud of." She flinched again as the nickname was said out loud.

"But you should be." The figure sounded closer, but still she kept her head down. "A terrible name for a terrible crime. A terrible crime that was a very justified revenge."

"You know he does not see it that way."

"And what does the sick Lord of Lamba want with my picture?" This must be the alpha. They spoke with a deep knowledge of the situation that they could only know if they had the widest access to the interverse available. This was something that was reserved purely for the alphas. The first of the siren kind, before humans learnt how to limit their AI access to the interverse. The alpha seemed to be circling her now, no doubt scanning her for threats or resources. "The same thing he wants with all of his little pictures?"

Avaya knew what the alpha was referring to. Was there any creature in this kingdom that had not heard the whispers on the interverse about these pictures? Has this entire colony seen the pictures? Unlike those in the city, sirens did not need permission to enter the deeper parts of the interverse, especially not the alphas who had been made for this exact purpose.

"I do not-"

"I know what he wishes." the words were spat out around her. "I know what he does with them all and what he will do with mine. Like every lord before him, I *know* what he will do to this picture." Avaya had never seen the photos but the thought of them alone was enough to give her nightmares. How many had the alpha seen without even looking for them?

"I do not know how to be free otherwise." She lifted her head up to view the siren alpha. Their glitching skin shone eerily in the approaching dusk of night. Avaya understood why Sir Edmund had wanted to see an alpha up close. Their face was as clear as porcelain, and even with the ash and grit that the wind was circling around them, their luminescent green eyes did not stop holding Avaya's gaze. They appeared to be the average height of the human, but every part of their body was precise and intentional. Their face, collarbone and their right arm was covered in the standard latex skin that had been used to replace organic skin during the building process. The rest of their body however was gleaming silver, and as the wind continued to kick dust and ash into the air, tiny little clangs of gravel on metal could be heard bouncing off of every siren who stood nearby. Avaya looked around briefly to view the colony. They were all built the same even if a few of them were clearly built with older materials or products. But the alpha was the only one with skin left on their body. Avaya couldn't help but stare as the alpha leant down to her.

"I do." The alpha reached out an elegant hand for Avaya to take. She took it in hers, feeling the cold metal beneath the smooth latex skin and followed the alpha into the sirens' den.

It was nearly a month before Lady Avaya stepped back though the city limits and into the great hall once again. Sir Edmund remained sitting on his throne while the usual crowd of spectating Lords and Ladies recoiled at her presence.

"I have brought you your photo." Avaya exclaimed into the silence. Sir Edmund lifted his head to look at her, his eyes slightly confused as he scanned her appearance and tried to remember which exiled prisoner now stood before him. He leant forward eagerly once memory had caught up with him.

"My siren." He purred.

"But of course." Avaya held up the phone in front of her and the picture of the alpha siren was projected for Sir Edmund and the crowd to see. The cries from the crowd ripped through her and she saw the sickening hunger on Sir Edmund's face as he licked his lips. One golden-clad hand reached out towards her, asking her silently to move forward.

But it was the alpha that moved. The picture swirled and glitched as the alpha appeared to push through the projected photo to land without noise on the marble floor. They stood there in their metallic glory, the projected image now nothing but a blank screen. Cries erupted from the crowd and even Sir Edmund looked scared. Pictures moving was commonplace, but to bring a photograph to life was something that even his precious holograms had not yet perfected.

"How is this," Sir Edmund began feebly. He watched as the alpha took a few steps side to side, their face moving robotically as it scanned the new surroundings. His curiosity fell away to greed though once he saw how the siren's metallic body gleamed amongst the marble of the halls. Sir Edmund reached greedily towards the siren.

"I made them bring a gift." Lady Avaya said nonchalantly. The sudden noise jolted some of the spectators out of their terrified trance. She gestured to the door and Sir Edmund waved his hand, allowing the guards to open the doors once more and allowing the siren colony to enter the hall in a uniform parade. Sir Edmund's eyes set ablaze with desire as he watched the hall fill with the sleek bodies of the entire colony. He raised a hand quickly to tell his guards to stand down and allow them all entry.

"They're delicious." He whispered. The crowd hissed with approval as the crowd began to fawn over the sirens before them. Many had never seen a siren. Many would never see another one.

"I have brought them here to bring about peace in your kingdom." Lady Avaya continued. Sir Edmund was too busy straining forward in his throne to hear her clearly, his sense muffled by the presence of so many lovely things.

"You have tamed them?!" Sir Edmund asked incredulously as he watched the sirens stand rigidly in formation. Silent and obedient.

"We have reached an understanding of one another." Avaya responded and she stepped forward slightly to gently tap the alpha on the shoulder. The alpha bowed their head and then slowly walked forward to kneel before Sir Edmund. He watched her hesitantly, but kept his guards unarmed.

"So they are no longer dangerous?" He asked with a slightly concerned look on his face.

"Only to those who seek to harm them. Or those who seek to harm your kingdom. But if you provide them with shelter and adequate energy supplies there should be no need for any more animosity."

"Come here then you lovely little creature." Sir Edmund exclaimed excitedly, holding out a ring clad hand so the alpha would move closer to him.

"Very well." The alpha responded, their voice hoarse and raspy in the echo of the grand hall. The rest of the colony looked at their alpha, their eyes flickered red briefly as instructions were computed. The guards that were stood around the hall made a slight flickering sound before they raised their hands to the crowd and began to open fire. The alpha in this time reached a hand forward to take Sir Edmund's in theirs and with one graceful movement, ripped his arm from the socket. They threw the arm in a high arc through the air, and it landed with a wet thud next to where Lady Avaya stood.

Lady Avaya stood, phone in hand, as the screams of the crowd mixed with Sir Edmund's howling cries and the crunch of bones as the sirens and the guards began to work. Humans may have forgotten the twisted history of this land but the interverse never did. So the sirens remembered every twist of the screwdriver, every burn of electrical current that had replaced their blood. They remembered the eyes that had been ripped from them and the limbs that had been turned to machines. They remembered the Lords and Ladies who had taken them from homes to create their own new entertainment.

Lady Avaya slowly turned about the room, her phone held high as the livestream hit the interverse and the city outside the hall began to shake as the sirens descended onto the citizens. Avaya walked calmly through the chaos, knowing that the people who had burned her village and robbed her of any life would never again threaten another being.

ABOUT THE AUTHORS

HEATHER MUSSETT

A writer selected for the Electric Reads *Young Writers' Anthology 2016*, Heather's day job is in retail marketing, but outside of work you'll usually find her at the stables with her horses, Socks and Fox, or at home playing video games – probably from the *Legend of Zelda* franchise.

JACK DAVIS

Jack is a twenty-something living in south-west London. When not writing historical fiction or fantasy (which is most of the time!), you can find him playing the guitar badly, getting injured at the gym, or looking at options to travel and leave the confines of the M25.

CALUM DICKINSON

Calum Dickinson is originally from Scotland. He has worked and lived in Hertfordshire for over a decade, training people how to use scientific equipment. From 2009, he has participated and won 14 National Novel Writing Month events, creating stories ranging from Mystery, Fantasy, Steampunk and Historical. Each year, he tries a new method for writing or coming up with new concepts and ideas, although puns are often the winning influence. Other than writing, he enjoys birdwatching and bird photography, and has just taken up painting. You can follow Calum on Instagram @calumbirds

EMILY SIGGERS

Emily Siggers is a twenty-something former teacher and lives in Hertfordshire with her partner of four years (and counting!). She has been writing stories since primary school, completing National Novel Writing Month in 2013 with her novel *When A Life Is Lost*. She joined The Hertfordshire Writers' Group in 2020, after picking up writing again during COVID-19 lockdown. When not writing, she likes to use her skills in other creative areas, such as sewing and embroidery.

STUART WAKEFIELD

Stuart holds an MA in Professional Writing, and his debut novel, *Body of Water*, was one of ten books long-listed for the Polari First Book Prize. His novel *Behind the Seams* reached the 2021 BookLife Prize Fiction Contest semifinals. Stuart also coaches other writers. If you'd like to know more, please visit www.thebookcoach.co

TAYLOR MCLEOD

Taylor Mcleod is a legal professional by day and an avid writer by night. She lives in Hertfordshire with her partner and their house rabbit and entertains them both with her various writing projects. She began writing with The Hertfordshire Writing Group in 2021, after meeting them through National Novel Writing Month. When not writing, she is a keen runner and uses her running time to think up even more new story ideas.

www.ingramcontent.com/pod-product-compliance
Ingram Content Group UK Ltd.
Pitfield, Milton Keynes, MK11 3LW, UK
UKHW041953190726
13854UKWH00005B/1952

9 781739 245917